Wouldn't change a thing

Dear Reader:

Mental illness can be a topic that is swept under the rug, especially when it comes to family. Such is the case with Antoinette "Toni" Williamson, who deserts her mother for decades while living and promoting the lie that she is deceased. When the truth is splattered on the front page of the local newspaper that her mom's actually institutionalized, Toni's life in Atlanta begins to crumble. It affects her design business and her relationship with her fiancé, Lamonte, and she flees to her hometown of Sparta, Georgia for comfort. However, there she discovers more secrets await her and meets challenges once she reconnects with her mother.

Stacy spent summers in Georgia listening to stories told by relatives on her porch, and now she creates her own provocative tale told through the eyes of Toni. Readers will enjoy a connection with the main character and her family members in this bittersweet journey that sheds light on mental health.

As always, thanks for supporting the authors of Strebor Books. We always try to bring you groundbreaking, innovative stories that will entertain and enlighten. I can be located at www.facebook.com/AuthorZane or reached via email at Zane@eroticanoir.com.

Blessings,

Zane

Publisher
Strebor Books
www.simonandschuster.com

ALSO BY STACY CAMPBELL

Forgive Me

Dream Girl Awakened

ZANE PRESENTS

Wouldn't change a thing

A NOVEL

STACY CAMPBELL

STREBOR BOOKS

NEW YORK   LONDON   TORONTO   SYDNEY

Strebor Books
P.O. Box 6505
Largo, MD 20792
http://www.streborbooks.com

ISBN 978-1-59309-598-7
ISBN 978-1-4767-7729-0 (ebook)
LCCN 2015934629

First Strebor Books trade paperback edition July 2015

Cover design: www.mariondesigns.com
Cover photograph: © Keith Saunders/Marion Designs

10 9 8 7 6 5 4 3 2 1

Manufactured in the United States of America

For information regarding special discounts for bulk purchases, please contact Simon & Schuster Special Sales at 1-866-506-1949 or business@simonandschuster.com

The Simon & Schuster Speakers Bureau can bring authors to your live event. For more information or to book an event, contact the Simon & Schuster Speakers Bureau at 1-866-248-3049 or visit our website at www.simonspeakers.com.

This book is dedicated to Sparta, Georgia.
Without you, there would be no stories, fond memories, or history.
To all my teachers from Head Start through college who endured my
fantastical dreams and interesting ways, thank you. There is a special
place in heaven for you. Also to my furry friends Marcus Kinchlow
and the late Lady Marie Williams, your presence provided a great
source of inspiration. Finally, to my late childhood neighbor,
Mrs. Elizabeth Carr. Thanks for always asking about me and
inspiring me to keep writing.

Then

"Let's face it; everyone in life is passing for something."
—*Woodrow Guill, Sparta, Georgia*

Clayton Kenneth Myles is my father. That's my story and I'm sticking to it. Well, Clay and his partner, Russell Morris. They are two of many factors that always made me the odd girl. The one with two dads. The one with the rickety family tree.

Clayton whisked me to Atlanta on my ninth birthday; April Fool's Day in 1984. I'd made a yellow cake in my Easy Bake oven, and before I could lick the milk chocolate frosting from my fingers, Aunt Mavis told me to go outside and play in a tire swing until my ride came. She joined me a few minutes later in the opposite swing, wearing her white nurse's uniform.

We smiled at each other and she said, "Hard decisions have deep consequences." She stood and gave me a tight hug. "This will make sense when you get older. We're doing this because we love you."

A speeding, shiny, black Chrysler Laser interrupted my "What do you mean?" The car topped the hill with a plume of smoky dust chasing its fender. The car skidded to a halt, and out jumped Cousin Clayton, a high school English teacher and the family grammarian. Tall, pencil-thin, and rubbing an immaculate goatee, he looked at us, his dark eyes misty from crying.

"Honey, have you heard the news?" he asked Mavis.

"What's wrong?"

"Cousin, Marvin Gaye is dead! His father shot him in the chest earlier today. The grapevine—no pun intended—is saying he was strung out on cocaine and spending hours watching porn videos in his bedroom. He was wearing a maroon bathrobe he'd had on for days. He was convinced someone was going to kill him. I told Russell something wasn't right when we went to Marvin's last concert, but he wouldn't confirm or deny anything," said Clayton, peppering the rehash with sweeping hand gestures. His purple, short-sleeved cotton dress shirt and tie were soaked, as if he'd run a marathon, and his black slacks were equally wet. Clayton and Georgia heat were archenemies.

"Oh my," said Mavis, clutching her chest. "What a waste of talent. I bet Russ and the other sound engineers are devastated. I know how you love your entertainers and how much you love Russ's studio stories." She gave him a suspicious gaze. "Do you remember the terms of our agreement?"

He eyed me swinging. Her words had jolted him back to the purpose of his visit, his mission. "We have her room decorated in pink and white." To me, he said, "You're going to love your canopy bed and dolls. I found some beautiful dolls on my last trip to India. It makes no sense for a little black girl to be in love with those hideous, pug-faced Cabbage Patch Kids."

Mavis grabbed Clayton's arm and they walked near the hydrangeas. I eavesdropped, caught fragmented utterances floating in the air. Georgia Mental Hospital. Paranoid Schizophrenia. Mall episode. Long recovery. As they leaned into each other, they stole glances at me and shook their heads in pity.

Mama was home one day, gone the next. I knew she wasn't dead. Death always ushered in visitors, fried chicken, potato salad, and a slew of relatives who only appeared for funerals or when spoils were divided.

"Toni, go inside and get your suitcase," said Aunt Mavis. "You're going to Atlanta to stay with Cousin Clayton a few months. You'll be back in time for school in September."

"What about my classes?"

"Clayton pulled some strings. You'll be in a magnet school until June."

I peeled my body from the swing and ran to my room. My jelly shoes squeaked and a small breeze lifted my sundress. I zipped my packed suitcase and thought of my older sister, Willa. Last year, Mama sent her to live with our aunts, Norlyza and Carrie Bell. After making me test the food Willa prepared, Mama said she was poisoning our food with arsenic and d-CON pellets. I stepped onto the porch, suitcase in my left hand, Dream Skater doll in my right. I tiptoed into the middle of the adults' conversation.

Clayton looked at Mavis. "So when is Greta coming home?"

"It'll be a while. Raymond and I have to nurse her back to health again. We can't keep her at the house, so she's at the hospital. She's flushing her meds down the toilet."

"Do you think the episode had something to do with the divorce?"

"Hard to say. You know Greta has blue genes," said Mavis, winking at Clayton.

"Blue genes, indeed," he said.

"Mama has lots of blue jeans," I added. "I want the picture of her in the tank top and Lee jeans. I loved the checkered dress I wore. Daddy was grinning and Mama had that half-smile on her face. I sat between them on the motorcycle in that picture. Remember, Aunt Mavis?"

"How could I forget? That particular cookout is one of the happiest recollections of my brother before he…" Her voice trailed off with the memory.

"What a cute suitcase," said Clayton, lightening the mood. I followed him as he placed it in the backseat.

Aunt Mavis tightened my ponytail holder and hugged me again as I sat in the car. She closed my door and made Clayton promise to call her when we arrived in Atlanta. Clayton pulled down a pair of Ray-Bans from his sun visor. I caressed Dream Skater's hair.

"You ready, Antoinette?"

"Yes, sir. I'm ready."

"Don't be nervous. This is temporary until your mother gets better. You're with family, so there's nothing to fear."

"I'm not scared. I'm excited."

"That's the spirit."

He slid a bubble wrap container in my lap.

"What is this?" I opened the container and flipped the cassette tape over twice. It read *UNRELEASED*.

"Our little secret. Russ smuggled this out of the studio. Sent it two weeks ago when he was out in L.A. doing studio work on Marvin's latest album. Personally, I don't think this little ditty will see the light of day now that he's gone, but we get to hear it before the rest of the world."

With that, he plopped in a cassette and we drove away listening to Marvin Gaye extol the sanctified lady saving her thing for Jesus. We became a dynamic duo that day, Wonder Twins passing for straight and sane, heading to Atlanta munching honey-roasted peanuts and drinking ice-cold Coca-Colas.

Now

"Every morning I wake up clothed and in my right mind, I feel all right."
—*Lillian Stanton, Sparta, Georgia*

Chapter 1

Threes. It always comes in threes. How else can I explain my fiancé, Lamonte, knocking on my backdoor, my cell ringing repeatedly, and a slew of reporters standing on my front lawn at seven in the morning? I'm not cut out for this. Not on a regular day and certainly not the morning of my engagement party.

"Baby, let me in," says Lamonte.

His voice is so sexy he can talk the habit off a nun. I crack the backdoor open and my heart melts when I see him. During the spring and summer months, Lamonte ditches his suits in favor of starched collared shirts, chinos, and spit-shined oxfords. He holds my gaze, not showing any emotion.

"Lamonte, please tell me what's going on," I demand. I motion for him to come to the patio as I slide the door open.

"You haven't said anything, have you?"

"Said anything about what? Is there something you haven't told me? Is this about the Midtown project?"

Lamonte takes my left hand. I follow him, all towering six feet four inches of him, and sit on his lap at his favorite table in my house in the breakfast nook. We'd picked this one out together on a trip to St. Simons Island last year.

"Toni, baby," he says, rubbing my left hand and massaging my right shoulder. "This has nothing to do with me. It's about you. Actually, your family."

"Is Clay in trouble?"

"I think you should take a look for yourself, Toni."

I take a seat across from him now as he unfolds the *Atlanta Journal-Constitution*. There I am on the front page beneath the caption, "Mother Longs for Reunion with Daughters." Not only does the caption knock the wind out of me, but the accompanying photo leaves me momentarily speechless. It is a replica of the one I keep tucked in the bottom drawer of my home office desk. My sister, Willa, and I wear matching pink and black turtleneck sweaters. Mama had jumped up from her spot next to Willa and me at Olan Mills Studio that afternoon. She refused to pose with us when the photo was taken; she said the people in the camera lens were making fun of her.

Lamonte moves closer now, knowing I have to take in every word, examine the train wreck the *AJC* has created on what is supposed to be one of the most memorable days of my life. He waits for my full explanation. I can't offer one right now. His phone rings, startling us.

"Take it in the living room," I whisper.

I continue reading, thankful I closed my shades last night. Even in this dimness, I feel naked. I look at the photo again and my heart aches for my mother.

Lamonte returns to comfort me again.

He sits back and rubs his clean-shaven face. "That was Richard on the phone. He said the paper will issue a formal apology to you by noon today. The picture was supposed to be in silhouette, but went to print with full exposure. Don't panic, baby. Not now. We'll get through this together."

Richard Phelps, our mutual attorney, pokes fun at people so much we call it his side hustle.

"That's easy for you to say. The *AJC*'s readership and my colleagues all think I'm a garden variety fruitcake." I pause. "Did you say 'together'? As in, we'll go through with this engagement party and wedding?"

"Toni, I made a commitment to you. This doesn't look good, but I want to give you a chance to respond to what I read this morning." He holds up the article.

"How am I supposed to respond?"

"Start by telling me the truth. Please."

"Lamonte, Clay has the answer for everything. But you and I both know he's in no position to answer right now."

He motions for me to sit in his lap again and I enjoy resting there for a brief moment. I feel like a fraud in his arms. I'm trying to find the right words to justify my lies, but I can't. This wasn't a white lie; this was more like a pastel one, the kind you tell when you know the truth will get in the way of your happiness.

"Toni, this is awkward. I'll cook while we strategize."

In Lamonte Dunlap fashion, he goes to the kitchen, raids the cabinets, and starts his usual Saturday morning ritual the two of us enjoy when life is simple and we're not talking business and politics. He pulls down the Krusteaz pancake mix, grabs bacon and eggs from the fridge, and finds my bag of oranges so he can squeeze the life out of them the way we like.

"We have to think of something to say to the reporters. I'll call the Blue Willow Inn to let them know we're still on for the engagement party," he says as he plops eggs into the pancake mix.

"Light on the eggs, Lamonte." His back is turned to me, but I know his mind is moving at lightning speed. He hunches his shoulders as he stirs the mix. "You're about to face more scrutiny than you have in your life. Are you ready?"

"I don't want to be bothered with this today."

"I'll step out on the lawn after we eat and address the scavengers."

"Yes, after we eat," I say.

Lamonte prepares our plates and pours juice. "Everything will be fine. This will blow over before you know it."

The elephant in the room grows. My hands tremble and my knees bounce as I think of an explanation. I've lied so long I'm not sure what the truth looks like.

I sigh and ask, "Aren't you curious about the article?"

His face slackens as he sips juice. "If you want to explain, that's your choice. I find it hard to believe the woman I've loved the last five years would keep a secret this huge from me. I'm waiting to hear what the mix-up is."

Ouch. I face the man I love. The one I've only allowed a tiny glimpse into my world.

"I meant to tell you before the wedding, Lamonte. The opportunity never presented itself."

"You were willing to have a wedding without having your mother present?"

I nod.

"What else should I know about you? You told me your mother died."

I shift in my seat. My cottony mouth offers, "I was young when I moved to Atlanta. My family thought it would be good for me to have a break from my mother's episodes."

"Episodes?"

"She—"

Lamonte's phone rings again. The voice announces Brooklyn Lucille Dunlap. Lamonte answers on the second ring. He accidentally presses the speaker button—a knack I can't get him to shake—and his mother yells, "Where's the lunatic?"

Lamonte quickly takes the phone off speaker and steps away from me. I can't hear everything she says, but from her booming voice, I string together, "bad choice," "not wife material," and "crazy grandchildren."

Lamonte holds up his hand and says to his mother, "I'm a grown man capable of making my own choices. Goodbye, Mother!"

He joins me at the table again, picks up the *AJC*, and re-reads the article. I see disappointment in his face and reach across the table to caress his hands. He pulls away.

"For twenty-three years, you've lived in this city without driving a few towns over to see your mother who's institutionalized in a mental facility?"

"Lamonte—"

He reads from the article. "My family decided it was better to parcel my children out like land just because I lose my grip on reality sometimes. My own baby girl is a big-time architect in Atlanta and she won't come to see about me."

"Lamonte—"

He holds his hand up again and reads, "She is so ashamed of me she spells her business name like a man. She won't use the name me and her father gave her."

"Lamonte."

"Toni, you told me the reason you spelled your name *Tony* was because you didn't want to be discriminated against as a female architect."

"That is true. When people see the name Tony Williamson, they assume I'm a man and are willing to do business with me. Tell me you haven't noticed the shock in men's faces when they meet me for the first time."

"Toni, you've been in business five years. Everyone in Atlanta knows Tony Williamson. Your work defies gender. Even race. Who are you? Don't I deserve to know who I'm about to spend the rest of my life with?"

I've got nothing. There is nothing I can say to him to convince him how sorry I am.

"Did you ever try to reach out to your sister all these years?"

"I tried. No luck." I'll fix this lie later.

Lamonte clears our plates from the table in silence. A die-hard penny-pincher, he rarely uses my dishwasher. Says it's too expensive. Instead, he fills my sink with hot water, Dawn, and a capful of bleach and cleans the dishes. As if his scrubbing will wash away what is going on between us.

I join him at the sink, but he shoos me away, tells me to get ready for tonight. I gaze out the front window at my lawn; a few reporters remain.

I walk to my front door, yank the door open, stand in my robe and slippers and yell, "You are trespassing. Please leave the premises."

Chapter 2

After Lamonte leaves, I swipe a casual outfit from my closet and run to the office to pick up a few items I left last week. Most of my personal and household items are at a storage unit on Virginia Avenue. The drive from Atlanta to Conyers isn't far, but Lamonte and I decided it would be easier for me to move into his house before the wedding. I have a few items at his place, but next week, I'll move the bulk of my storage contents to his house. Our house.

My home is a management company's dream: hardwood floors, fresh paint, a new roof, stained-glass windows, and exotic tile. Nothing says 1930 meets 2007 like modern upgrades. After five unsuccessful attempts to find a renter, I struck gold with an Atlanta Art Institute student. After a credit check and three separate creep-ups on her current apartment, I presented Giovanna with a lease. I think of her as I enter the building. This is where I first met her.

My hope is no one notices me as I dart in and out. I'm down to five to-dos on my party checklist for tonight. I can't stop trembling, and my stomach is in knots over the party. How many people will show after reading the article? How will Lamonte react when someone brings up my mother?

Phillip, the doorman at my office building, opens the door for me and tips his hat, but averts his eyes, a first for him. I speed up, hoping to get this done and get out of the building ASAP.

I place a picture of Clay, Russell, and me in Cancun in a large box on my office chair. This will be one of the photos I place on the family portraits display at the Blue Willow Inn this evening. I gather up a few more items and check a few emails before leaving the office. I suspended work emails on my phone because I disconnect when I leave this place. Lamonte taught me how to unwind, kick up my feet once I step away from computer drafts. I log on and the first email I read takes my breath away.

Dear Ms. Williamson:

Due to recent findings, we regret to inform you that your donation to Daughters Alone will be returned to you within the week. Furthermore, your invitation as keynote speaker at our annual empowerment series has been rescinded. We cannot expose the girls to someone whose idea of motherhood is tainted and shrouded in lies. The girls looked up to you and even went out of their way to comfort you after learning your mother died in a plane crash when you were their age. We appreciate the time you've given the girls thus far—workshops, career day, tour of your firm—but the revelation that your mother is alive and well, albeit in horrific circumstances, makes it impossible to continue the mentorship agreement we have with you. I wish you well in your future endeavors.

Dr. Erin Crawford, CEO, Daughters Alone

I stare at the screen. Of all the work I've done in the community, mentoring with Daughters Alone has been the most rewarding. I pick up the phone to call Dr. Crawford and notice the email arrived at six o'clock this morning. She probably read the article after the paperboy tossed it on her porch around four-thirty. She boasted of being a zombie until her morning fix of coffee and the *AJC* kicked in.

As I hang the phone up, Kimmie Foster's face comes to mind.

She was most smitten with me when I joined the girls for the Orange Hat Tea at Restaurant Eugene. I didn't get the orange hat reference until Dr. Crawford said orange represented the sunset, a new start. The girls, all left motherless by death, drugs, or abandonment, needed encouragement, hope for a better day. Kimmie sat next to me at the tea wearing a cream-colored Sunday-go-to-meeting suit that hung off her thin frame. I knew I'd purchase her new outfits with Dr. Crawford's permission. She pulled at the coffee-colored stockings that resembled elephant wrinkles and crossed and uncrossed her skinny legs. She tried to hide her scuffed, cream-colored shoes by keeping her feet planted under the table. She was silent during the tour of my office, but at the tea, she leaned in to me and said, "You're lucky your mama died. She couldn't help it. My mama didn't want me and I don't think my aunt does either."

I sipped sweet tea, remembering Dr. Crawford told me Kimmie's mother couldn't handle child-rearing responsibilities and walked out. "Kimmie, she has to get herself together. I'm sure she'll be back when she's ready."

"How did your mother die?"

Until Kimmie asked, I never offered specifics. I sipped again and said, "She died in a plane crash when I was nine."

Kimmie's eyes locked with mine. "I'm sorry, Ms. Toni. I'm sure she's in a better place."

The sad memory of Kimmie's eyes jolt me back to my emails. A string of emails from prospective clients inform me next month's meetings are canceled. All of them. They read the same. "Due to unforeseen circumstances." "Decided to go in a different direction." "Found a comparable price with another firm." The last one started with the words "integrity" and "character." I shut the messages down because I can't deal with this now.

Clayton Kenneth Myles's life rule number one states, "Get through tough situations with a smile and a fierce poker face; you can collapse with tears and a bowl of Mayfield Butter Pecan ice cream later." Clayton Kenneth Myles's life rule number two states, "We are superheroes with the following letters on our chests: *CLD. Cry. Lie. Deny.* Pick one that bests suits the jam you're in." I'll have to use rule number one tonight. It's the only way I'll be able to face our friends and my future in-laws.

At least I have Lamonte's love and commitment. I've saved money over the years and can weather a financial storm if I can't get new clients. Instead of a week for a honeymoon, Lamonte and I scheduled a month off to get adjusted to being husband and wife. I can count on him to comfort me until the wedding. He is my rock, the one person I've grown to depend on over the years.

I gather a few more items from my office and head to the lobby. I slightly trip on the newly buffed flooring and the contents of my purse scatter on the floor. I kneel, stuff the items back in my purse, and stop when I see my mother's photo. Willa surprised her in this shot, caught her off guard when she wasn't taking her meds. The wild look in her eyes reminds me of the times she anesthetized her pain with heart-wrenching soul tunes. Bill Withers was her Thorazine. Marvin Gaye was her Prolixin. Natalie Cole was her Haldol.

She stares back at me, the spitting image of her mother, Rose. I adjust my face with a smile so the pain doesn't show. As I exit the building, Philip, eyes still downcast, bids me farewell. I wave to him. I turn once more, hoping our eyes meet as they always do. He gives me a sympathetic nod. A few spaces from the building, I find a bench, whip out Mama's photo, and look at her half-smile, the one she flashed when she wasn't medicated.

Chapter 3

My most prominent memory of my mother's psychotic breaks is one that happened at the Hatcher Square Mall in Milledgeville, Georgia. We stood near the wishing well water fountain filled with pennies. I'd just thrown in two pennies and prayed to the mental illness gods. I begged them to stop the voices my mother heard at three in the morning. She argued back and forth, assuring them she was a good person and a suitable parent. She scratched at her arms and scalp some mornings, pulling plugs of hair or making zigzag lines in her skin. Their accusations were many; she defended herself against each one.

Near the fountain, she ripped open a pack of Kools she had hidden in her pants pocket and lit one. She looked at each passerby and asked me, "Don't you hear that bitch talking to me?"

I turned to see if a woman had tried to get our attention.

My mother popped the collar of her starched white shirt. "She's got one more time to call me out my name."

A security guard approached us. "Is everything okay here?" He pulled a radio from its holder on his wide belt.

She gave him a vicious once-over. She pointed her finger at him and beckoned him to come closer. "What do you think? I know you hear her too."

Nervous, I chimed in, "Officer, everything is fine. We're going to Strawberry Suds and Dreams."

I guided her away from the fountain, upset that I'd left the house alone with her and without her medication. We were supposed to get perfume and then chicken breast sandwiches from Chicken Delite once we returned home. Only Aunt Mavis could calm her down in these instances. This episode had carried over from last night and I needed a way to get her out of this mall. Mama pointed to Strawberry Suds and Dreams before I could direct her attention to the exit.

We walked into the store as she muttered curses to the invisible woman stalking her. She lifted her hands, dropped them, and said through clenched teeth, "I ain't doing it!" As cool as you please, her attention shifted to Hannah, a perky salesgirl pitching soaps and lotions at infomercial speed. Pink and red mister in hand, she moved toward us with a reserved smile.

"Hi, would you like to try our strawberry mist? Today's special is buy two, get one free."

Mama extended her left wrist to the young lady, whose pitch quickened with her interest. "It's a light mist and part of the Strawberry Suds and Dreams Relaxation Collection." She tossed shoulder-length curls to the left.

Mama ran her wrist under her nose. She shook her head, then insisted we leave. "I told you I don't have a gun!" she shouted.

Hannah inched away from us to the register. She picked up the telephone and asked security to come to the store. I pulled Mama's arm toward the store exit. Hannah's call would trigger the worst in my mother and we had to leave. She dashed my hopes when she dropped to the floor, Indian-style, and beat the floor with her fists.

Her voice raised two octaves, startling shoppers who formed a small circle around her. "You can't make me kill President Reagan!"

She bushwhacked the floor until blood trickled from her hands.

The same security guard from the fountain broke through the circle of onlookers. He radioed nine-one-one, and a woman in the circle pulled me into her warm embrace. While others whispered, she knelt beside me and said, "I'll be with you until the ambulance comes. Don't be scared."

"Can you call my Aunt Mavis?"

"I'll find a pay phone and call after they take your mother. I can't leave you here by yourself."

She stood with me as paramedics entered the store with a gurney. Mama fought them with all her might, looking past me and my guardian angel. I panicked as a needle appeared and the male paramedic shot my mother's left arm with precision. She lay still as they hoisted her on the gurney.

"Where are you taking her?" my guardian angel asked the paramedics.

"Georgia Mental. What can you tell us about her?" he asked.

I spoke up. "She hears voices. She didn't take her meds."

"Sounds like skits," said the female paramedic. I watched them take my mother away. After sifting through her purse for change, my guardian angel found a pay phone and called Aunt Mavis. Her lips were moving, but I heard nothing as people passed us. They pointed at me, pity covering their faces. Minutes later, we were seated at the fountain again.

"Your Aunt Mavis is on her way from Sparta."

I silently rested in her bosom again.

"I know what you're going through. I work at Georgia Mental and some of my people are a little touched, too. We don't talk about it much, though."

"Why not?"

"The world ain't got sympathy for people that's different." She rubbed my back. "You really don't know me, do you?"

I shook my head and asked, "You're from Sparta, too?"

She considered my question as she touched the sparkling chain looped around her stylish glasses. "I'll let your Aunt Mavis tell you who I am."

Chapter 4

The June weather is perfect and the engagement party crowd isn't as thin as I anticipated. I'm surprised so many people are here. Their smiles are tight and their congratulatory hugs limp, but they're here. Their presence says they have faith we can weather this storm. Lamonte and I greet our guests on the Blue Willow Inn lawn. I look at the stately mansion and marvel at how my vision was transformed perfectly. The staff worked with me and recreated all my design sketches. Gazanias, begonias, and African marigolds are placed throughout the yard and on the steps in hues of red, pink, and gold in Tuscan planters. The Reed Thorne Jazz Band plays our favorite selections on the left side of the wraparound porch. The far end of the lawn is set up for our engagement party games. We zigzag through the maze of waiters and waitresses indulging our guests with champagne, cheese and bacon-stuffed mushrooms, pesto sriracha shrimp and basil bruschetta, fruit, cheeses, and julienned vegetables.

We shared our second date at The Blue Willow Inn; our first date was at my house putting out a small kitchen fire I started trying to cook Lamonte's favorite dishes. I doused what was supposed to be smothered chicken and smashed potatoes with my kitchen fire extinguisher. The cream cheese pound cake stuck to the pan because I didn't realize the pan required Baker's Joy, and the yeastless rolls refused to rise. The following Saturday, we drove here to Social Circle and Lamonte politely said he didn't mind cooking, but if our relationship continued, I'd have to master a few staples.

"You'd better let me see that ring!" a weak voice calls from the right.

I turn my attention to the cupcake bar. Decked out in matching seersucker suits are Russ and Clay. Russ's suit is green, Clay's, blue. Lamonte falls in step with me as I approach them. I bend toward Clay's wheelchair and he makes a brave attempt to sit up, but falls back and coughs.

"Careful, Clay," Russ admonishes and places the oxygen mask on his face.

Clay takes in a few bursts of oxygen, then removes the mask. "Honey, I wouldn't have missed this party for all the cocaine in Columbia."

"Or all the inside trader secrets from Wall Street," Russ added.

The four of us laugh as Clay coughs again. Emphysema halted his teaching career, but his jokes are endless. His vanity made it nearly impossible for us to make him wear the mask instead of the nasal cannula. He swore he was cuter in the cannula and felt the mask obstructed his handsome face.

Clay makes slight moves in his chair. He wants to dance, but his body is unwilling. "Is that what I think it is?" He hums in time with the band's vocalist. It isn't until Russell matches his humming that I remember the song.

"Mysterious vibes, that we share. God's love is in the air. We'd know the Blackbyrds anywhere."

As if chasing away a memory, Clay silences Russell with a finger to his lips. He smiles at me. "Hold your ring finger out for me."

I place my left hand in his as he turns the ring around, observing every detail as he did my clothes and shoes when I was younger.

"Now *that* is the princess of all princesses. How exquisite." He faces Lamonte. "Who designed it?"

"Premier by Divine."

"Brother, that's good taste."

"She deserves the best." Lamonte strokes my back.

Clay looks up at Russ. "Maybe we'll get hitched when this backward state changes the laws."

"Keep dreaming."

Russ gives me his famous head-to-toe sweep. "You are wearing that dress, Toni. Cream is your color, girl! I know you'll be an even more beautiful bride."

I twirl so they both can take in my fitted lace minidress.

Russ's attention zooms in on my neck. "You still have the necklace, I see."

I touch my cream, sparkly bib necklace and remember his sacrifice. The night of my senior prom, Russ placed Roxanne—his name for the necklace—around my neck as he waited with me for my prom date. Darren Bennett never showed. I later learned Darren's father said his son "wasn't going to no sissies' house to pick up a date." Russ held me his arms as I cried myself to sleep that night.

"I only wear it on special occasions."

Russ touches my stomach and I readjust my belt. He shudders and removes his hand as it trails the lace.

"That dress and necklace might be nice, but your hair," said Clay. I touch my flowing locks and strike a model pose for him. "Design Essentials ain't nothing but the devil! You held out until college, then you messed up all that pretty hair. I wished you'd stayed natural."

"Clayton Kenneth Myles, you know I had more hair than Rapunzel. I couldn't do anything with it. Besides, Lamonte likes me this way. Don't you, baby?" Lamonte nods.

Clay touches the hem of my dress and struggles to speak. "Toni, I'm sorry about the story in the *AJC*. Maybe it's a sign that you need to—"

"No!"

He tries again. "Did you at least invite Willa to the party?"

"Her invitation was returned unopened. Can't say I didn't try."

He takes my cue to drop the subject and rotates his wheelchair a quarter-turn to face the cupcakes. "Chocolate sprinkles, please," he says over his shoulder to Russ.

Lamonte, oblivious to our secrets, says, "Let's go speak to my parents."

I look at Russ and Clay again, marveling at their thirty-year union. Clay, thinner, bald, and fifty-three, is running out of seasons. Russ, strapping, confident, and ten years Clay's senior, continues to be the rock of their relationship. As a sound engineer, he continues to do studio work around Atlanta and lend his expertise to up-and-coming sound afficianados in his basement studio. He mixed sounds with heavy hitters when I was younger, and I loved hearing stories from his concerts. I walk away from them, proud they are my role models.

Brooklyn Lucille Dunlap is holding court with several of our guests. Lamonte's father stands off to the side and lets his wife take the lead as usual. He watches as her arms move in stride with her story. "Pick an island, any island in Hawaii, and imagine me enjoying myself so much I fall asleep in the sun. As if I need—" She stops when she sees me. She reaches out to Lamonte without acknowledging me. "Come here, my precious son."

Her stature looms as large as her personality. She runs her fingers through her pixie cut and adjusts her cleavage in a black, fitted jumpsuit. This is her affront to my cream-or-white attire request for the ladies. Lamonte holds me closer and she relents.

Brooklyn clears her throat and motions to a woman standing near her. I recognize the towering woman from Lamonte's photos. This is his Aunt Karen. Brooklyn and Karen could be mistaken for twins, but everything about Karen screams earthy. She had followed instructions and wears a beautiful, one-shoulder cream dress that stops just below her knees. She sweeps me into a bear hug and almost picks me up.

"I'm Karen. Welcome to the family, Antoinette. We've talked on the phone a few times, but nothing beats meeting face-to-face. I'm glad Lamonte found the love of his life."

I smell more than champagne on her breath. Clay taught me how to mix a mean Rob Roy. Karen may as well have said, "Smell that scotch and sweet vermouth, don't you?" She releases me and I regain my composure. "It's nice to meet you as well, Ms. Karen."

"Call me Aunt Karen. You're practically family." She whispers in my ear, "Don't you let my high-faluting sister bother you. Everybody's got crazy running in their family tree."

Lamonte sees my face flush and intervenes. "Aunt Karen, where is Uncle Hunter?"

"Still in Jersey. He had some business to handle, but he'll be here for the wedding in October." Karen flags a waiter, takes a champagne flute, and sits on a white bench.

"What did she say to you?" Lamonte asks me.

"Baby, it doesn't matter. We promised each other we'd get through this, and we will."

He plants a kiss on my forehead as a colleague waves to him. "Be right back. I'm going to speak with Stan Mitchell."

As he walks away from me, I run to him and whisper one of Clay's favorite sayings in his ear. "Look at the swing on that back porch!"

He shakes his head with a playful smile and continues. I speak to a few more well-wishers before I head to the games area. On the way, I feel a slight jerk on my arm.

"Let's speak in private for a moment," Brooklyn says.

"I'm going to check on the—"

"I said a quick minute!"

I follow her to the back of the restaurant, gearing up for a war of words. Whomever said respect your elders didn't know Brooklyn. She's always been terse with me. I never say the right words, wear the right clothes, or use the right utensils.

She spins around before we reach our destination. "I've had it up to here with all of this!" She makes a wide, circular motion with her long arms. "The only reason I'm here today is because Senior insisted we honor our son's wishes. But I will never accept you as a daughter-in-law. Ever!"

"You don't have to accept me."

She points her long, manicured nails in my face. "Idiot, when you marry someone, you marry their family as well. Their history and their struggles. Unfortunately, you bring too much to the table. My son deserves better, and her name is Christina Garrett."

Christina's name is a sucker punch. Though Lamonte and Christina were on the outs when we met, he said they broke up because she was on the fast track to becoming Brooklyn 2. Brooklyn 1 felt a woman's place was beside her husband, not in the workplace. Christina was willing to put her impressive credentials on a shelf to be Mrs. Lamonte Dunlap, Jr. To birth his tall sons—the Dunlaps are boy breeders—and keep his house. I always have and will continue to make my own money.

"My independence is what Lamonte loves about me."

"He'll grow tired of a neglectful wife soon enough."

"Christina doesn't have the ring, I do. Now, if you'll excuse me."

She shouts at my back, "I give this marriage a year, tops. He'll toss you in the wind like the confused trash you are. Bad enough you have a crazy family, but living with those…homosexuals."

"Listen—"

The jazz band dies down and I hear Lamonte's voice speak into a microphone. "Toni, where are you, baby?"

I roll my eyes at Brooklyn. "We'll continue this later."

I continue to the front lawn, and to my surprise, the crowd has gathered in a large semi-circle in front of the restaurant. Lamonte has taken the microphone from the vocalist and he beckons me to join him on the front porch. I smirk at Brooklyn who takes her place next to Aunt Karen and Senior.

Chapter 5

A man assists me as I climb the steps and stand next to Lamonte. He pulls me close again and my pride swells at the way he gazes at me. I hold his hand as his eyes scan the crowd.

"When I was thirty-one, I met the woman of my dreams. I never thought I'd find a woman to complete me. The last five years with Toni have been magical."

Take that, Brooklyn Lucille Dunlap!

Russ and Clay are closer to the porch now. The times they interacted with Lamonte were always positive, and they literally gave their stamp of approval. Russ created a T-shirt with Lamonte's picture that contained a circle and the words *Russ and Clay-approved.* I wore the shirt to bed when I spent the night at Lamonte's house in Conyers.

"Antoinette Willamson is phenomenal. If the virtuous woman in the book of Proverbs had a photo, it would be a picture of Toni, her face beat with MAC, wearing a flirty dress by Angie and Carlos Santana wedges, and cleaning our place top to bottom. Now, the cooking…"

I punch his shoulder as our guests laugh.

Russ yells, "That's our girl!"

Lamonte pulls me closer and his heart thumps. I rub his back in hopes he relaxes. I breathe in his Versace Man and wonder how I snagged such a good guy. Loving, forgiving, and responsible. He responds to my soft pats by facing me. A slight tremor in his right hand challenges his grip on the microphone. He caresses my face and turns to our guests again.

"To sustain the magic of our union, Toni and I have decided to postpone our wedding at this time."

Brooklyn mouths *Thank you, Jesus* to Senior and Karen. They look as shocked as I feel. My Spanx close in on me and I feel them tighten. A collective gasp fills the air and my plastered smile fades as I grab the microphone.

"What he means is—"

He snatches the microphone back and gives me a sharp, fall-in-line expression. "We wanted you to hear this from us instead of others. We plan to work through our difficulties and ask for your thoughts and prayers."

He drops the mic and heads toward his vehicle in back of the restaurant. Our guests whisper and I spot Clay cupping his oxygen mask. I chase Lamonte to the back of the building and catch him as he dips into his SUV. Several guests join us to witness the sideshow. I pull on his door, but not fast enough. He locks it.

I tilt my face close to his. "Lamonte, why go through with this if you weren't sure?" I will tears not to fall, but they are noncompliant.

"Why lie to me for years if you love me?"

"Lamonte—"

"Mom can handle things here. I'm leaving."

I spot a huge bottle of Absolut next to his wallet on the front seat. He revs his engine and barrels out of the parking lot. Russ appears like a ghost to comfort me, but I'm too furious to accept his reassurance. I spot my vehicle and dash. Russ gives chase.

"Toni, stop!"

I call over my shoulder, "Why?"

"You're in no condition to drive. Calm down. You can talk to Lamonte later."

I yank my door open and pop the trunk. My forgetfulness has cost me some lovely bags, so I always keep my purse in the trunk when I travel. My routine is a godsend today.

"Toni—"

"No one makes a fool of me!"

Russ touches my shoulders. Our eyes meet and he understands. "Do what you have to do."

I pull out of the parking lot toward I-20 West. Lamonte's home is thirty minutes away, so I have time to gather my thoughts. He is going to face me like a man and tell me something! Through my tears, I eye our giveaway CD case on the floor. Our engagement photo serves as the cover. We created this memento in January as a party giveaway, compliments of Giovanna. I pick it up and flip the case to the list of love songs that represent our romance. Atlantic Starr's "Send for Me." Brian McKnight and Vanessa Williams's "Love Is." Marvin Gaye's "Sunny." I toss it back on the floor and veer onto the interstate. V-103 is what I need to soothe my nerves. The CD love songs will only make me cry worse and beg. Not happening today.

My best friend, Jordan, would be my shotgun rider if she weren't in Italy on business. I can see her pulling her long locks behind her ears and cursing Lamonte like he stole something. She would have blocked him at the Blue Willow Inn parking lot and made him explain himself. Theirs is a love-hate relationship I enjoy watching. She couldn't make the engagement party, but threatened me with death if she wasn't my maid-of-honor. I want to call her, but embarrassment fills me. I can't dial her number. She'll probably reject me when she returns to the States and realizes her ace is an impostor.

I spot Lamonte's X5. I speed up and pull alongside him, hoping to get his attention. His head bops, and I know he's tipsy and listening to music. I blow my horn. He looks at me, adjusts his Bluetooth, and switches lanes. I follow suit, tailgating to irritate him. This doesn't work either. His arms thrash as he leans to the side. This is his pose when he talks to Brooklyn. I'm sure she's soothing her poor baby and congratulating him on keeping the family tree unpolluted. I pull back a few spaces, realizing he's heading home. I'll keep my cool until we get to my second home, or at least what I called my second home.

We make it to the subdivision entrance in record time. He coasts through the gate and I wait my turn to go past the massive, wrought-iron fence. As I punch in the code, I notice a Georgia State Trooper behind me. I ignore him at first, then panic. He's following me. I pull into the driveway, anxious and horrified at the sight on the front porch. Lamonte stands mountain tall, arms folded. He looks at me with disgust as the trooper approaches us.

The officer takes off his hat and addresses me. "Ma'am, Mr. Dunlap called and said you are stalking him. He asked that you be escorted off the premises."

"Since when is coming home with your fiancé stalking?"

Lamonte gestures to the items on the porch. I look at the boxes and see my clothes, shoes, design software, and souvenirs from past outings.

Mrs. Porter, Lamonte's neighbor, strolls across the lawn, wrapped gift in hand. "Toni, Lamonte, is everything okay?"

The site of a state trooper would surely have the Woodland Hills tongues wagging. I'm sure she means well, but Lizzy is the neighborhood gossip and thrives on drama. The neighbors call her Diahann Carroll behind her back because she is the actress's double. Today, bouncing, silver curls frame her flawless face. A trip to the makeup counter is her Saturday indulgence. She brushes her elegant, lavender dress with her hands and gives me the gift.

"I had every intention of coming to the party, but I got tied up with a friend. Please accept this gift as congrats on your engagement." She awaits a response from us.

"Thank you, Lizzy. I'm sure I'll love it."

She hesitates. "Well, I'll be going back inside now. I look forward to the wedding in October."

Lizzy walks backward toward her house, anticipating some action. She enters her garage and looks at the three of us once more before closing the door.

"Officer, would you please help Ms. Williamson load these items into her car?" Lamonte makes the word *Miss* sound like leprosy.

"That's not everything I have here. At least let me—"

Lamonte stretches his arms across the front door. "I'll ship the rest of your things to you. Just leave, Toni!"

I back away from this stranger. This is the thanks I get for investing five years of my life in a committed relationship. I know I lied, but I had my reasons. Lamonte promised me in the beginning of our relationship we'd work through everything. Sickness. Morning breath. Career moves.

I see Russ and Clay's stamp of approval T-shirt on top of my clothes box. I hoist the carton in my arms as the state trooper brings the shoes and souvenirs. Three steps into my journey, the voice of pre-emphysema Clay fills my head, saying, "Don't you ask that man another damn question! You are Antoinette Maria Williamson. I raised you to hold your head high and be proud!"

I nod at the words. I hear them, want to absorb them, but the box slips from my arms and everything goes blank.

Chapter 6

Greta

Mavis and Clayton were dead wrong for giving away my children like they did. They didn't discuss the matter with me and didn't care about my feelings, one way or the other. After one of my breaks at the Hatcher Square Mall back in the 1980s, they made the choice to separate the girls, claiming I was a bad influence on them. I didn't find out about Toni until after the deed was done. Who does that to someone? I was and still am capable of taking care of my children. I may be a resident of the Georgia Mental Hospital, but I have a right to see my children.

I know Mavis's saddity self is mad because I took my story to the *AJC*. What started out as a how-do-you-feel-about-your-treatment-here story turned into my personal rant on how family treats the mentally ill. Not that I'm mentally ill, I just get a little crossed up sometimes. The only reason I'm crossed up is the medication they give out around this place. They act like it's cotton candy at the State Fair. How is a person supposed to make rational decisions if you feel like you're floating on the moon all the time? Just call me Sally Ride and give me a white spacesuit, because some days, I don't know whether I'm coming or going. Wait, Sally's deceased. I'm sorry, Jesus, I didn't mean to mock the dead. I'm waiting. I'm waiting. Whew, Jesus just winked, nodded, and said the comment wasn't mocking Sally.

I took to hiding pills under my tongue and pretending to swallow them while the nurse is standing over me. Annalease, my room-mate, taught me that trick. I slip the pills in my pocket when the nurse turns her back. My latest drug is Depakote. I know I'm in trouble when they give me a pink one, because it renders me help-less and keeps my visitors away. Abilify, Remeron, and Haldol do the same thing if I take them on schedule. I get more visitors when I take the Zyprexa. I have three people who come to see me on a regular basis: Jesus, Mahalia Jackson, and Clark Gable.

I know the doctors and nurses make fun of me all the time when I say Jesus is with me always. The first time I shared my Jesus secret with Dr. Wells, he asked, "Do you mean Hay-Suess?" I looked him straight in the eye and said, "Jesus is a celestial being; Hay-Suess is Latino." I pointed to Jesus sitting on Annalease's bed. Dr. Wells said he understood, then upped my medicine dosage.

Don't you believe that carpenter mess. Jesus has a coat of colors, Brooks Brothers' suits, hiking gear, all kinds of clothes. Not once has he come in my room with bib overalls or paint-stained boots. He's a Renaissance man. He truly is everywhere at the same time. He comes through the window most days when he visits. Plops right down on Annalease's bed and asks me how I'm doing, if my arthritis is flaring up, how the doctors and nurses are treating me. He is my friend, indeed He is.

I fell out with Jesus when Paul left us in 1982. Felt like He ran for the hills and took His time coming back. Then I lost my teaching job. Then the house. Then the few friends I fellowshipped with from time to time. Then the children. In a span of nine months, everything secure in my life disappeared. I'm talking David Copper-field-poof.

Mahalia came to me different. She's been with me since 1980. Paul and I double-dated with Mavis and her husband, Raymond.

Mavis, a nurse and my sister-in-law, and Raymond, a stern military man, always entertained at their house. Plantation is more like it. All that acreage and a big, old white antebellum house that sits off from the road, begging for a horse and buggy to pull around the circular drive.

We had gone to a concert at Georgia College to see Rufus and Chaka Khan. I was shocked Mavis came out with us, since that wasn't usually her kind of entertainment, but she sipped a Bud light and swayed her bottle to Chaka Khan like the rest of us. She didn't want to go to the Blue Note afterward, so we went back to their house. She convinced us to watch movies, and before we could protest, she played *Imitation of Life*. Paul put his arms around me and stroked my hair as we watched the movie.

Before Mahalia sang, "Trouble of the World," she winked at me. Honey, she belted out that tune, stepped out the pulpit in that angelic black-and-white robe, ran her big hands over Annie's sparkling white spray and coffin, and came right out of the TV and sat on my left side. She told me not to tell Paul she was sitting there, said we had a few things to talk about regarding relationships. I got stiller than Lot's wife, because I didn't want to hear Mavis's mouth about medication or my hallucinations. Mahalia looked to her left and right like she was about to expose the world's biggest secret and told me to call her 'Halia. She said we had more in common than I knew. I winked back at her as assurance her secret was safe with me. I wasn't telling a soul she was with me. She still guides me through so many struggles. Turns out her marriages weren't perfect either.

Clark is a mystery. He'll come in my room, but he never talks to me. He'll stand back in the corner, coal black hair and mustache shining, and smile. That's it. I wonder who sent him and what they told him to tell me, but I can't get him to talk.

Back to my children. My girls are different as day and night. My baby girl, Antoinette, is my delicate flower. She's short with a little gumdrop nose and pretty brown skin. She puts me in the mind of those energetic waitresses who run back and forth from the kitchen getting lemon wedges and extra bread for customers. She's a peacemaker, always wanting everybody to be happy. Smart as a whip too. She cheered me up when I had my moods. I taught her how to braid hair, and when I'd fight with Paul, she'd grab my red-and-green jar of Royal Crown grease and find us a spot in front of the den TV. She'd part my hair, scratch and grease my scalp, and faster than a cat could lick his ass, my hair would be in these chunky French braids. Mavis tried to help me teach her to cook, but she was always up under me, like she was scared something would happen to me if she closed her eyes. The best she mastered was the Easy-Bake Oven. She never could get the hang of slinging cast-iron skillets and Dutch ovens.

We had Fish Fry Night every Thursday. Paul, a cabinetmaker, stopped by Macklin's Seafood on Milledgeville Highway to pick up catfish, perch, and hushpuppy mix. I kept potatoes on hand for French fries. I cleaned the fish outside at a table Paul made for me and brought it back in the kitchen to marinate for a while. While I washed and dipped that fish in my secret seasoning blend and special meal, I'd walk back and forth to the den and watch Paul, Willa, and Antoinette dancing. Paul fired up the record player and always played Antoinette and Willa's favorite song, "Sunny." If you ask me, Bobby Hebb's version was better than Marvin Gaye's, but they wouldn't listen to me. Beats me what was so special about Marvin's rendition, but they danced like they were at a family reunion.

I don't have much to say about Willa. I told you my girls were night and day. Antoinette was day, Willa was night. She wasn't fat, wasn't skinny. I guess you could say she was attractive, if a woman like her turns you on. I'm saying woman because she was fifteen when I last saw her. She started smelling herself and sassing me when she turned fourteen. Can you believe I overheard that heifer telling Paul to keep an eye on me because she was worried about me? Told him I had been talking to myself and hearing voices. She wasn't slick. She told those lies to get Paul on her side so she could sneak out with Larry Watkins, her chemistry tutor. Paul was dumb enough to believe her and started monitoring me. He'd pop home from a cabinet job just to see how I was doing after I lost my teaching job. He wasn't slick either. I know he was doing that on his way to his other woman's house. I can't prove it, but I know it in my heart.

The last I heard, Willa was married with a daughter and living in Birmingham, Alabama. I thought about reaching out to her, but then I recalled the Roundup herbicide she put in my oatmeal and mashed potatoes, the arsenic-laced sweet tea, and the D-Con pellets she mixed with my brownies, and I decided to leave well enough alone. But she is my child, and I deserve to see her again. I've been aching for both of them lately.

The best years of my life were spent in the home-house. A woman is supposed to make her house a castle. That means keeping it together and being open to letting people stop by if they need rest or comfort. I kept the house ready for my family, but I also kept it together for Jesus. Think about how it says in the Bible, "He stands at the door and knocks." Do you really think Jesus wants to come in a house stepping over dirty underwear, half-eaten food, or roach droppings? Let's not talk about dirty windows that haven't been scrubbed.

I tried keeping everything together before it slipped away from me. I had to leave the home-house and move into a place downtown called the Drummer's Home. It was a long waiting list to get in, but Queen Mavis waved her magic wand and I got an apartment. I kept it neat as a pin until the mall incident. I'm not blaming anyone for what happened, but the woman who told me to kill President Reagan had been after me long before the mall. She climbed in the window at night whispering to me about the deed, she came through the gas oven unit, and she followed me back and forth to school when I was teaching. I believe she is the reason I lost my job, because she reported back to Principal Jones all that was going on in my home. Who else would have told him about the D-Con pellets, the fights with Paul, and the trouble I had keeping the girls in check?

I miss my children. Sometimes, I miss Paul. I don't know how much longer I have left on this earth, but it would be nice to touch the girls, to see how they've grown up. I wonder if my grand-daughter took after me or Paul. I wonder if they think of me. Annalease is like a daughter, but she can't substitute for Antoinette and Willa. I know I'll see them again. I know it in my heart.

Chapter 7

Lamonte changed his mind. As he licks my feet like a four-course meal, I thrash about with a pillow over my head. I toss and turn, glad to be conscious after the blackout. He realizes how ridiculous it is to throw away our years together. I grab the sheets in anticipation of the make-up sex. He flicks his tongue between each toe, a slobbering, repentant fool. I love him more for his desire to make things up to me. My eyes tighten as I picture him in his red briefs with the Angelina Jolie pucker I bought for Valentine's Day. If only I had the negligee he bought me. We could start this make-up party right.

Softly, I say, "Lamonte." I wait for him to acknowledge me. "Lamonte."

"Whiplash, no!" a woman's voice yells.

I fling the pillow from my head and scream. A black Cocker Spaniel like Brooklyn's barks and retreats behind the woman.

"Whiplash, sit!"

The dog makes a circular motion and obeys her. Through a fog, I see Aunt Mavis. I untangle myself from the sheets.

"Aunt…Mavis? What am I doing here?"

"Calm down, Toni."

"Don't tell me to calm down! Why am I in your house? What the hell?"

She calls for backup. "Raymond, please come help me!"

My uncle's footsteps fill the hallway. He stands in the doorway and blushes at the sight of me. He turns away and says, "May, I'll come back when she's decent."

I look down at my pink oversized pajama set from Lamonte and cover myself again.

She clears her throat. "That was the only night set in the box. I got them from the backseat of your car. You refused to put on the T-shirt I gave you. You've been resting for the past two days and I planned to take you to Milledgeville today for more clothes."

"Two days?"

I go to the mirror and Whiplash follows me. I look like highway road kill. My hair is matted and my breath smells like a can of sardines. I get a whiff of my underarms and curl my nose. Whiplash isn't bothered by my odors and licks my leg.

"Whiplash, enough!"

I sit back on the bed and place my head in my hands. I'm back in Sparta again. I survey the room. This is where Willa and I spent our early years eating popcorn and Girl Scout cookies and watching movie after movie, reciting lines until we fell asleep. This house was *the* happening spot when we were young. Cousin Clayton had a wife then, Uncle Raymond and Daddy manned the barbecue grill like pros, and Aunt Mavis and Mama sat around like schoolgirls, laughing at jokes and swapping nursing and teaching stories. Our girly room has been converted to a modern, chic bedroom. The twin beds have been replaced with a modish bedroom set and bold African prints line the walls. Although I'm funky, I inhale childhood smells—Johnson's baby powder sprinkled beneath the sheets and Aunt Mavis's secret liquid washing detergent mix. Mama begged for the secret, but Aunt Mavis's lips remained sealed. Aunt Mavis's homemade potpourri fills the room. She sits next to me and rubs my back.

"I'm sorry about everything that happened, Toni."

"Tell me how I got here so I can leave."

"Russell called. You collapsed at Lamonte's place and he thought maybe you needed to come home a while. I gave you a mild sedative to help you rest."

"Atlanta is my home."

"That's obvious." She stands to retrieve my cell phone charging on dresser.

"What does that mean?"

Aunt Mavis sits again and shows me my cell phone contacts. "ICD? Really?"

My face flushes. The typical call-my-family-I'm-in-trouble code is ICE—In Case of Emergency. However, I knew I didn't want to see my relatives in this town again unless I was dead. Hence the code ICD: In Case of Death. The only exception to my rule of never coming back here is that Ingram Brothers' Funeral Home handle my arrangements since they buried all our relatives.

"Toni, do you hate us that much?"

"*Hate* is a strong word."

"I know your life hasn't been conventional, but we thought—" She places her hand on my shoulder.

"You thought?! Do you know what my life has been like all these years?"

I yank my shoulder from her grasp. Whiplash follows me to the closet and I open it, searching for a clean outfit. *Damnit, I'm not at home.*

"You need to rest a while, Toni. Things have spiraled out of control. Recuperate with us."

I spin around. "Recuperate? You separate me from my mother, she puts Willa and me on blast, and now I'm supposed to act like nothing happened?"

"Our doors have always been open. *You* decided not to keep in touch with *us!*"

Checkmate. For years, Aunt Mavis and Uncle Raymond reached out to me with cards, calls, and gifts, but I had rebuffed their olive branches.

"Are the towels still in the same place? I want to take a shower and go home."

"Russ said you rented out your home."

"I can ask her to leave. I don't want to be a burden to you and Uncle Ray."

"You're not a burden, Toni."

"I can't tell. I seemed to be a *really* big burden twenty-three years ago."

Aunt Mavis and Whiplash disappear from the room and return with a facecloth and towel, Lever 2000, and a toothbrush and mouthwash. "You know where the bathrooms are. Take your pick."

"*Thank you.*" Aunt Mavis isn't moved by my nasty tone and extends the wash items.

"Your keys and cell phone are on the dresser. I handwashed your lace dress."

I snatch the plush bathing items and pad down the hall as Whiplash whimpers. I sniff the towel and facecloth and smell her mix. Daddy said Aunt Mavis learned her hospitality skills from my paternal grandmother, Helen Williamson. As I trudge the hallway to the bathroom, Aunt Mavis's spring-cleaning ritual surrounds me. The walls give off the minty smell of peppermint and almond oils. The hardwood floors gleam with a high gloss, windows are streak-free, and a table near the bathroom houses *Good Housekeeping*, *Ladies Home Journal*, and a decorative bowl of Mary Janes, Coconut Long Boys, and mini boxes of Nerds. I swipe a Coconut Long Boy and think of Willa. I put it back in the bowl. These candies were the holy trinity of sweet treats for us and the cause of our childhood dental visits. So many memories, so few of them that I want to embrace.

I slam the bathroom door, angrier at myself than I've been in years. I have to get back to life as I know it. My heart is broken, my business projects are dry, and I'm mad as hell that, overnight, my life is gone. This is only a slight setback. I can turn this around. I can flip the script and make this tragedy work for me. I got myself into this; I can get myself out.

I jump in the shower, tracing my steps and assessing how I got here. Until now, I never believed in karma. Not only is karma real; she's a woman scorned who'll stop at nothing for payback. I should have never agreed to be featured in *Atlanta's Movers and Shakers*, a monthly show featuring area professionals under forty. I had devised a brilliant plan—my appearance would garner exposure for Williamson Designs. Reality shows, movies, and design festivals are Atlanta staples; I wanted in on the action. I hadn't anticipated the going-back-to-your roots approach the reporter took. Of course, I couldn't say I was from Sparta, Georgia. That would open the door for more questions.

Clay couldn't deny my account, so I pulled out the big guns. When Mindy Barlow asked if my mom and dad were proud of my accomplishments, tears fell like raindrops. Taking her cue from Barbara and Oprah, Mindy produced a box of Kleenex from thin air, plucked several from the box and handed them to me. She waited as I dabbed my eyes. I hunched my shoulders, leaned forward, and cried like I'd lost my best friend. She seemed pleased with herself for tugging at my emotions as my chest rose and fell with each shudder. Mindy nodded with empathy as I recounted how hard life had been without my parents.

See, that's a pastel lie. Not white, but just enough color to be believable. When she prodded for more details, I waved my hands in the air as if the pain was unbearable. She cut to commercial with childhood photos of Willa and me. The appearance reaped astounding benefits. I received more inquiries and social media hits in three hours than I'd had in years. Respondents said they felt a connection when they saw the pictures. That was my biggest hiccup: the photos. How could I have been so stupid? I waited for fact checkers to out me. I waited for someone from Sparta to say, "Humph, that's Paul and Greta Williamson's daughter. They ain't a bit more dead than Matt Lauer. She oughta be ashamed of herself." I thought I'd gotten away with it since no one had said anything. But karma worked her magic overtime.

Whiplash scratches at the door, pulling me back to my present mess. I hear low whimpering, then a loud bark. This is my cue to blow this joint and get back to my house in Atlanta. If I get started soon enough, I can do damage control. I stop the twin shower head action, pat my skin dry, and lotion up with Aunt Mavis's hand-made Lavender Lush. Her home is still an organic dream, with handmade soaps, lotions, and detergents. Uncle Raymond encouraged her to sell her wares and turn her hobby into a business, but she only sold them during Sparta's annual Pine Tree Festival.

I complete my hygiene business and exit the bathroom. Whiplash follows me to the bedroom and sits on the bed as I gather my things. She scratches herself as I look at her. Her dark eyes beg me to stay. Even though fury fills me, there is still warmth and love in this room. The dog follows me as I head to the front door. Aunt Mavis works on a needlepoint project while Uncle Raymond reads *Stars and Stripes*. I eye the craft box. A retro, black-and-white telephone is today's project.

She tosses the telephone aside. "Toni, will you please sit down a moment?"

I sit across from her on the loveseat. I stare at the box again. Aunt Mavis always had a thing for different projects. No cats, dogs, or roses for her.

"Yes, ma'am."

"Why are you running off so fast? Stay here awhile, until things cool off."

"Stay here and do what?"

"Unwind. Regroup. I'd love to see you reconnect with your mother."

"Reconnect or connect, since you gave us away?"

"Enough, young lady!" Uncle Raymond folds the paper as perfectly as the creases in his starched pants. "You will not speak to my wife in that tone."

"Ray."

"No, Mavis. I've watched her lie all these years and pretend we never existed. Cards, gifts, and letters always returned to us unopened. Never a thought or consideration as to why we did what we did."

Whiplash is as surprised as I am by Uncle Raymond's loud voice, and she retreats to a corner. Aunt Mavis scoots next to him on the couch. "Ray, we should explain ourselves to her. We owe her that much." His furled brows soften as she speaks.

They're still the picture of calm and solidarity after forty-eight years of marriage. Whenever my parents fought or my mother had an episode, May and Ray—my parents' name for them—came to the rescue. Uncle Ray's military sternness ruled the household. A retired lieutenant colonel, his was an ironhanded regime. May was the fire; he was the ice.

He accepts her gentle admonishment and addresses me in a quieter tone. "You don't need to go running off again. Stay here with us. We'll explain everything when the time is right."

I stand, careful not to disrespect my beloved uncle. "I appreciate your kindness. I want to be alone for a while. I promise I'll be back to sort things out."

They stand now, both enveloping me with love. Whiplash joins in the group hug and laps at my leg. I gather my things and stack them on the porch. Whiplash makes small circles near colorful potted marigolds. I take the steps two at a time, marveling at how Willa made me sweep while she pulled weeds from the flowerbeds that still line the yard. I pop my trunk and toss in my engagement dress. I'll sell it on Ebay when time permits.

Panic fills me as I eye the boxes from my eviction in the backseat. The finality of my relationship with Lamonte is etched on the boxes in his handwriting. *Do not return.* I will myself to move forward as I start my engine and creep out of May and Ray's driveway. They become small dots as I watch them in my rearview mirror. If I drive fast enough, I can make it to Atlanta and be back in my house before sundown and help Giovanna move her things.

Chapter 8

My neighborhood got its turn at gentrification bat seven years ago. Downtown Atlanta is the place to be for excitement. The traffic is hell, but the people watching is amazing. I'm proud to call the Mechanicsville area home. I'm five minutes from downtown, Turner Field, my office, and sites of many dinner dates with Lamonte. I swing a right on Garibaldi Street and examine several properties. I check for sale signs, patrol the streets for neighborhood characters, and insert my design ideas on lawns with sparse or abandoned landscaping.

Fifteen minutes into my drive, I pull into an empty driveway to calm my breathing. This is a tradition I shared with Lamonte every weekend. As with any routine, I've fallen into it without a second thought. I close my eyes and see Lamonte getting excited as we drive down street after street discussing Plan D. He said smart couples didn't rely on plans A and B; you had to anticipate life all the way through Z. We'd comb this area for properties, discuss the purchase and flip of them, then sit back and mentally count our money. We opened the D&W account together at Bank of America and funneled money once a month for the past two years. We planned to start D&W properties three years after our marriage and when the account reached $125,000. Clay expressed his disdain about D&W properties with the statement, "No ring, no financial commingling. Simple as that." We were off to a good start with $75,000. *The money.*

I plow out of the driveway to the nearest Bank of America branch. My clammy hands grip the steering wheel. The Lee Street branch is the closest. I make it there in record time, swerving as I nearly hit an elderly woman on a cane. She rakes her fingers over a chignon bun and leans on her cane. She looks at me, flicks her middle finger, and points her cane in my direction. "Slow down!"

I wait until granny drives off in her Crown Victoria to enter the bank. *Please be here. Please be here.*

I enter the bank in panic mode and I'm greeted by a dapper young banker. "I'm Keith Justice. How may I assist you today?"

Words fail me and I'm motionless. Keith instructs me to follow him. I take a seat and catch my breath.

"How may I assist you today…" He pauses a few beats for my name.

"Toni. Toni Williamson. I'm here to check my account balance."

I fumble through my purse for my ID and the account number. If Lamonte left half the money, I'll be grateful. I slide my ID to Keith and recite the account number as he punches away at his keyboard. He tilts his face toward the screen. "Whoa!"

My heart palpitates as he turns the screen toward me. I stare at the amount. One hundred and twenty-five dollars. *"Bastard!"*

Keith's eyebrows do a Groucho Marx. "Bad break-up?"

"Bad is an understatement."

Keith investigates further and scrolls through the account history. "Appears the withdrawal was made early Saturday morning. Lamonte Dunlap received a cashier's check in the amount of $74,875." I sit back in the seat and ponder my next move. "Would you like to close the account, Ms. Williamson?"

"Yes. Please."

I wait as Keith retrieves the last of my money and places it in an envelope. "Is there anything else I can do for you today?"

"No. You've been most helpful."

I exit the bank, enraged by Lamonte's cruelty. He thinks so little of me as a person he didn't even want to give me one percent of our goal. I'm not even worth one percent? Not a tear will fall from my eyes today.

I look in the mirror and declare, "I am Antoinette Maria Williamson and I will survive."

I open my purse to stuff the envelope inside and notice handwriting on the back.

You don't deserve this situation. Keep your head up, Beautiful. KJ.

Keith's note makes me smile.

I head home and imagine how wonderful a hot bath will be. My knees and hands tremble as I drive. Half of that money was mine. I'm in good financial standing, but thirty-thousand plus is thirty-thirty plus. Period. Good thing I'm a homeowner. A man is the last thing on my mind, and Giovanna can find another place. This is the A, after all. Properties abound. I'll break the news to her gently. I will return her deposit, first two months' rent, and give the money back with interest.

Giovanna instructs two men carrying a decorative dresser as I park in my driveway. Her flowing hair blows in the slight breeze as she waves her arms toward the door. The yellow sundress she wears makes her look fifteen instead of twenty-four. Her bronze skin says Sao Paulo. She's a true Brazilian girl.

She spots me and runs to my car, pearly whites sparkling. "Ms. Toni! *Como estamos?*"

I lean from my window. "Giovanna, *Não falo português.*"

She bends to face me and her hammered, gold-spiraled nose cuff glistens. "Well, you spoke that phrase I taught you. How are you, Ms. Toni?"

The two men go inside with the dresser. "I thought you'd already moved your things in."

She opens my door, awaits my exit, then hugs me. I feel her appreciation as she presses me close. "My dad and brother arrived from Sao Paulo Sunday, so we're moving the last of my things in now. Mom's inside. I want you to meet her."

I follow Giovanna up the stairs and I'm welcomed into my own home by the most delicious smells. My eyes beeline to the kitchen as a middle-aged version of Giovanna rocks her hips to a samba tune in snug jeans and a hot-pink fitted tee. Her hair, like Giovanna's, flows down her back and over the apron string tied around her neck. Her hot-pink leaf sandals sit next to the dishwasher. Immediately, I think of my trip to Rio with Lamonte. She hums along with the tune as Giovanna lightly taps her shoulder.

"*Mãe, Esta é a minha amiga*, Toni."

The tap startles her mother and she grabs her chest, wipes her hands on her apron, and extends her right hand to me. "*Boa Tarde. Coma Vai?*"

Giovanna translates. "She says good afternoon and how are you?"

I shake her hand and recall phrases Giovanna taught me when she frequented my building on her photography projects. "*Estou bem, obrigada.*"

She turns to stir the contents of the Dutch oven and redirects her attention to me. "*Você se junte a nós para o almoço?*"

"Mom wants to know if you'd like to join us for lunch. We're having coxinhas and feijoada."

"Sounds delicious. What is it?"

"Coxinhas is like a chicken croquette and feijoada is black bean stew."

I remind myself this isn't a social visit. "May I speak with you in private in the basement?"

Giovanna speaks a phrase to her mother and we head downstairs. I sit on her furniture and marvel at how quickly she's made my space hers. She joins me on the couch.

"Is everything okay, Ms. Toni? Is it the money? My mom and dad want to pay the rent each month, but I'm doing well with my photography gigs right now."

"What's your major again?"

"Photography is my side hustle, but my major is Digital Film-making and Video Production at the Art Institute. I'd love to edit videos, maybe work for a television station someday. With all the studios cropping up around here, I'm sure I'll find something."

I clear my throat. "I stopped by because things have changed with my situation."

"Wait? Did you move the wedding up? I knew Mr. Lamonte wouldn't wait until October to marry you. I could tell during the engagement photo session how much he loves you. You eloping?"

The unintentional punch hits me to the core. "I...um...the wedding is off for now. So, I may need to—"

"No! What happened?" Giovanna slips next to me in little sister mode and wraps her slender arm around my shoulder. "Luis and I look up to you guys so much. Please tell me it's a short break and not a final one."

"We won't be getting back together. It's for the best."

"Oh."

I look around at the basement again and see how Giovanna has transformed the walls with her beautiful photographs. The most striking photo is one of Luis standing in front of Emory University. Giovanna calls Emory his mistress because his days and nights are spent maintaining A's so he can get into medical school. They both spoke of making their parents proud when they had dinner with us. Lamonte thought it was would be a good idea to take the couple under our wing since my path kept crossing with Giovanna's. It's not fair to make her move because I lied.

"It's not the money, Giovanna." I search for the right pastel lie, since I don't want to toss her on the streets. "I've never had anyone rent the place and I want to make sure you take care of it. I've heard rental horror stories and this house is my baby."

Relief washes over Giovanna's face. "I'll take care of it like it's my own. I'll take better care of it, actually. Thanks for trusting me with your baby." She squeezes me tighter. "I thought you were putting me out."

"No. I know how close the house is to your school."

I stand to leave. Either Giovanna hasn't read the *AJC*, or she's unaware of the situation with my mom. For this I'm grateful. "I came downtown to check on my storage unit on Virginia Avenue. Since I was so close, I decided to swing by the house."

Upstairs, Giovanna's parents and her brother are enjoying lunch and engaged in lively conversation. I wave to them as she walks me to my car.

"I'll call you if any problems arise. Luis is very handy, but I won't let him touch anything without your permission."

"You know how to get in touch with me."

Giovanna hugs me again and walks back inside to her family. I get back in my car and plot my next move. Mama always called me delicate. The encounter with Giovanna made me feel spineless. Why didn't I kick her out, move back home, and close the blinds and eat ice cream day and night? Thirty pounds, a bad lace-front, and a drab wardrobe could make me a new person. I wouldn't have to explain anything and be brand new. I start my car as Giovanna runs down the steps with a P.F. Chang's bag.

"I forgot to give you this."

The bag contains lots of mail. I filled out a change-of-address form over a month ago for the Conyers house, but mail continues to arrive here. I scan a few bills, advertisements, and the latest issue of *Architectural Digest*. Hidden between the envelopes is a letter from the *AJC*. I open it and skim its contents. What good is an apology going to do now? I place the letter in the envelope and toss it back in the bag.

Giovanna peers through the front window at me. I bet her family is enjoying their meal, laughing, talking, and discussing how great it is to be one. A whole, intact family enjoying each other. I don't make it out of my subdivision without slamming my fists on the dashboard. I have no place to go and I can't believe I'm in this predicament. My engagement CD taunts me again. I place it in the changer and listen to "Sunny" as I ease onto I-75S. I'll find a hotel for the night and regroup. Being alone is the best thing for me. I change lanes and assess which downtown hotel I'll spend the next month having a pity-party. I can work from my room. Free Wi-Fi, room service, and cable television will soothe all that ails me. Someone out there wants my expertise; I just have to retweak my marketing efforts.

The traffic is worse today. Not only are cars creeping along on the interstate, I imagine a dignitary must have passed, because only a funeral procession would slow cars this much. I switch lanes again and look for the hearse. I can't believe my eyes. Not only is it not a hearse, but traffic is suspended by a white van. The sight of it makes me want to curse Richard Pryor under a table. Bold, black-and-green magnets affixed to the vehicle mock me—*Slow Moving Vehicle Due To Wedding Cake On Board*. Other drivers admire the van's careful delivery of its special guest. I wonder if the bride ordered buttercream or whipped icing. What fillings layer the cake? Strawberry? Key Lime? Chocolate? I look closer and see the bakery's name. *Let Them Eat Cake Bakery.* This was one of the bakeries Lamonte and I visited for wedding cake samples.

Try as I might, I can't concentrate anymore. Everything flashes before me like a movie as I drive. The 3D movie is of October and the wedding that will never be. Lamonte plants a big kiss on my lips after Pastor Worthen says, "You may now kiss the bride." Lamonte holds my hand as we jump our handmade broom. Lamonte carries me over the threshold of our home. Lamonte raises Lamonte Dunlap, III's glistening naked body to the sky and spins him around in a ritual of spiritual blessing in our backyard. Cookouts, double-dates, new contracts, and refurbished homes sail past me. I pull alongside the interstate and with shaky hands, I manage to dial Aunt Mavis's phone number. Her voice is like soothing waves at the beach on a clear day as she says hello.

I barely manage to speak. "Come. Get. Me."

Chapter 9

Uncle Raymond agrees to drive my car to Sparta. I wobble along as they help me into the passenger's side of Aunt Mavis's car. Whiplash laps at my legs again as Mavis motions for her to sit in the backseat.

"Are we going straight home or stopping for food?" he asks Aunt Mavis.

She looks to me for guidance.

"My storage unit is at the next exit. I need to get a few clothes. I'm not hungry."

Whiplash barks, shooting down my lack of hunger.

"We'll get you fries at the McDonald's drive-thru, Whiplash. Hold tight." Aunt Mavis pets her as she nestles in her booster seat. She removes a bag of treats from her purse and hands a few to Whiplash.

Uncle Raymond follows us to the unit. I draw a blank with my gate entry passcode, then remember it's a combination of my mother's birthday and my driver's license. I grab a few items, mainly clothing and one of my laptops, and get back in the car. Whiplash's panting is a nice distraction from my troubles. I've never been an animal lover, but something about her makes me feel like I have a friend.

"You can stay with us as long as you like, Toni."

"Aunt Mavis, this is temporary until I can get back on my feet. Maybe one month, tops."

"It will take you longer than that to get back on your feet. Home's been calling you for years."

"I didn't have a reason to answer then or now."

"Will you at least visit your mother?"

Beautiful trees and houses command my attention as I turn to the window. "It's been so long, Aunt Mavis. I don't know."

"At least think about it. I'm sure she'll be glad to see you."

Whiplash barks again as we near the next exit. "What's going on?" I ask Aunt Mavis.

She chuckles. "She sees the golden arches on the food sign for exit ninety-one."

"How'd she get the name Whiplash, anyway? That sounds like a male name."

"Your mother gave it to her on one of her short stints from the hospital. Your cousin Brenda's sons—"

"Brenda has kids?"

"Yes, ma'am. And a handsome husband named Charles. Anyway, we took a family trip to Callaway Gardens one weekend when Whiplash was a pup. The boys kept tossing her up and down and annoying your mother. She asked the dog's name and they shrugged. Your mother said, 'The way y'all throwing that dog up and down, she oughta be named Whiplash!' The name stuck and that's what we've called her ever since."

"I forgot how funny she can be sometimes."

"She is a lot of wonderful things when she takes her meds. I wish you would embrace that fact, Toni."

"I'll embrace that fact when you tell me why you gave us away."

The request silences Aunt Mavis. "You're too fragile right now. I promise you'll understand it all later." She rubs my leg as we pull into the McDonald's drive-thru.

Aunt Mavis's words ring true: my mother was lots of wonderful things when she took her meds. Before her diagnosis, I proudly rode to school with her each day. My mother's third-grade class ran out to greet her every morning. She coasted into her parking space at Sparta Elementary School, and before she opened her door, one student grabbed her piping bowl of grits sprinkled with butter and black pepper, one took her coffee, and one carried her briefcase inside. She favored pantsuits over dresses and skirts, unlike the other teachers. They fit her shapely frame. She walked me to my fourth-grade class and always waved to her fellow teachers in the lounge. By the end of my fourth-grade year, the waves and smiles became turned backs and snickers. I thought they were jealous of her, until a playground incident.

Lisa Jones, our class bully and Principal David Jones's daughter, gathered all the girls in a circle to play a game. We were her servants and she sat on her makeshift throne—a beanbag chair she brought from home—at recess every day. She kicked Annette Cousins in the back. Annette yelped and allowed her access to the middle of the circle. Satisfaction covered her face as she made us bend to her will. Her beaded braids clanked as she moved them to one side. Wielding a legal pad and a fat number two pencil, she sketched a picture of a house, and a mom with kids minus the dad. Above it she wrote, Whose Your Hollywood Daddy? My grammar flag flew at half-mast after she killed the usage of the word whose. Cousin Clayton had drilled the difference between whose, who's, there, their, and they're over the past few weeks. I snatched the pad, struck a line through the word whose, and replaced it with who's.

"Why did you do that?" she snapped. She snatched the pad back and looked at the new replacement.

In fluent Claytonese, I recited our latest grammar lesson. "Whose is the possessive of who. Who's is a contraction that means who is or who has. As in, who is your Hollywood daddy?"

"Oooooo weee, she told you!" said Annette as she high-fived three other servants.

Lisa pointed the pencil at Annette. "Shut up before I take your lunch money!" She shoved the pad in Annette's face. "Since you have so much to say, write your Hollywood daddy's name."

Annette scratched her head and scribbled *Eddie Murphy*. "My mama said he is so fine she wants to meet him."

"That'll never happen," said Lisa. "Your mama barely comes to the school for your PTA meetings, so how is she going to Hollywood?"

The sun glinted off the aluminum foil on the end of Lisa's braids as she passed the pad to Cathy. Cathy wrote *Michael Jackson*.

Lisa's face scrunched. "He's not going to let you live with those animals in his mansion."

"He could teach me how to dance, though. I could feed Bubbles and do things around the house."

Lisa waved off the notion and handed me the pad. I remembered Willa's crush on Dick Anthony Williams, but decided against listing him. The only reason she liked him was because Aunt Mavis thought he was handsome. There was only one man I idealized as a good father after my parents started having problems. He was loving, accepting, and made room for children that weren't his. He was a good provider and he was handsome. In all the reruns I watched with Willa, he solved problems and made sure the children were civil toward each other. The best part was that he worked at the house and in an office as an architect. He had drawings in a home office that he'd show the kids. His work even took them to Hawaii for a construction assignment. I wrote in capital letters.

ROBERT REED/MIKE BRADY.

Lisa laughed at my response. "You're not mixed. You can't have a white daddy!"

Another Claytonese phrase sailed past my lips before I could stop it. "Nuts are mixed, not people."

Lisa flipped the pad to the next page. "Just as well. You'll need a mother and a father soon, since your mother won't be teaching here much longer."

"What did you say?"

She dropped the pad, stood, and moved closer. "You heard me. Everybody's talking about how crazy your mother is. She can barely make it through third period without laughing and talking to people that aren't there. Why do you think she leaves at one every day?" She placed her hands on her non-existent hips and faced me, a grape Now-and-Later coloring her tongue. "The only reason my daddy hasn't fired her is because he's doing your Aunt Mavis a favor. Your aunt went—"

I reared back and punched Lisa in her mouth. BAM! She fell back, her head narrowly missing the monkey bars. I pounced her, slapping her face as blood trickled. I would move heaven and earth for my mother, and no one was going to disrespect her. Vickie Kendricks and Doris Hargrove pulled me off her while the other servants shouted, "Beat her!"

Mrs. Barnes, our teacher, took us to the office to face Principal Jones. He spanked Lisa and excused her. I rubbed my face from the one punch Lisa got in. Principal Jones gave me a cold compress and it soothed my face for a short time. Too embarrassed to face him, I dropped my head as he spoke.

"I'm very disappointed in you, Antoinette. I've never known you to fight. What got into you today?"

I shrugged. I looked at the photos of Principal Jones with his wife and Lisa. They seemed so happy. So normal.

"What did Lisa say to you?"

I paraphrased her words without thinking. "She said you said my mother is crazy and you're going to fire her."

Principal Jones made a steeple with his hands. His face reddened as he stood and came toward me. "Lisa said that to you?"

I nodded.

He placed a hand on my shoulder. "Lisa misunderstood a private conversation I had with her mother. Your mother is a valuable member of our school and we're doing what we can to help her. Everything will be fine."

"May I go back to class?" I asked, pressing the compress closer to my stinging jaw.

Principal Jones picked up the phone and dialed a number. He toyed with the abacus on his desk as he waited for the caller to answer. "Mavis, Antoinette isn't feeling well. Will you please come pick her up?"

I gazed out the window as they discussed other things and waited for him to hang up.

"I'm sorry for what Lisa said, Antoinette. My doors are always open for you. You're like a daughter, and if you need to talk about anything, I'm here to listen." He paused. "How has your mother been? How is your father?"

Clay and Mavis made me and Willa swear on Grandma Rose's Bible not to discuss anything about my mother or my father's difficulty caring for her. What went on in the Williamson household stayed in the Williamson household. Clay said people were like vultures, always swooping down to get gossip like it's a dead carcass. "No need to feed 'em the bird with your words," he said.

"She's doing okay, Mr. Jones. We're supposed to be taking a vacation to Florida this summer."

"I'm sure you'll have a wonderful time, Antoinette." He paused again. "How is Willa?"

"She's well." I looked out the window again and was relieved to see Aunt Mavis's Honda.

I knew she wouldn't take me home, because I had overheard Daddy saying he'd take Mama to her psychiatrist's appointment that day.

When I got home in the evenings from May and Ray's after Mama's appointments, Mama's catatonic state scared me but made me comfortable. She couldn't hurt us or say mean things. Aunt Mavis came into the office and greeted me with a hug and kiss for my boo-boo. She tossed the compress Principal Jones gave me in the trash and replaced it with one of the cold icepacks she kept in her freezer.

"Thanks for calling, David. I'll take care of her when she gets home."

"Don't make a big fuss. Lisa's mouth prompted this confusion."

"Oh." She looked at my face and motioned for me to go to the car.

I waited in the car as Principal Jones escorted her outside. Concern filled both their faces as they chatted. Principal Jones said something to her and caressed her hand. In return, she gave him a quick hug.

"Are you still allergic to the sauce on Big Macs?" she asks, drawing me back to the present.

"Ma'am?"

"Do you want something to eat or is your stomach queasy?"

Whiplash waits for my response as she nuzzles against me.

I face the canine. "Girl, when did you get out of your seat?"

"I'm taking her for a walk in a sec. She has to tinkle and move around."

"I'm not hungry. Thanks anyway. I'll eat later."

"Where were you, anyway?"

"The old days. Do you remember picking me up from Principal Jones's office after Lisa bullied me? How is he?"

"He died of prostate cancer about three years ago."

"Where is Lisa?"

"You mean Dr. Lisa Jones-Candler? She followed in her family's footsteps and is a professor at Stanford. She's done well for herself."

Wow. Even mean Lisa Jones found a husband. She probably tied him down and made him marry her. My stomach churns again.

"Aunt Mavis, do you have any aspirin?"

"Will Advil work?"

"Anything will do. Get me a small Hi-C orange, please."

Aunt Mavis places the order as Uncle Raymond pulls into a spot on the lot. She gets our food, parks next to Uncle Raymond, and gives me the medicine bottle.

"Give me Whiplash's fries out of the bag."

I pass the fries and pop the cap off the Advil. Whiplash barks louder for her fries as they exit the car. Aunt Mavis joins Uncle Raymond and they walk Whiplash around the parking lot hand-in-hand. I watch them and the way they communicate. Uncle Raymond smiles lovingly at her as she swats his hand away over something he said. I always envied their marriage and wanted my parents to be like them. I shared my fantasy with Clay once and he said marriages like May and Ray's don't happen overnight. He went on to say a lot goes on behind the scenes. Compromising and forgiving. Sometimes forgetting.

My phone tings. Jordan's text asks a familiar question since Saturday.

Did I do something to offend you? Please reach out to me.

What's there to say? I'm not who she thinks I am and I don't know how to make things right. I recline the front seat and let the Advil take effect.

Chapter 10

Aunt Mavis taps my shoulder and startles me awake.

"Where are we?"

"Good ole' Sparta, GA. You were beat. You slept all the way in."

I sit up and check my surroundings. I talk a good game about being a motherless child, but I loved my hometown when I lived here.

"Do you need to stop anywhere?"

"Not right now."

In the rearview mirror, I see Uncle Ray steering my car. He's keeping pace with the traffic about three cars behind. My old stomping grounds create a flood of questions.

Aunt Mavis reads my face. "A lot of your favorite places are gone."

"I see." A towering new high school sits off the road to my right. "When was this school built?"

"Late eighties, early nineties. It was a long time coming, and a welcome site."

"What happened to the old HCHS?"

"It's still standing. I can drive you by there, but it's a shell of what it used to be and an eyesore."

I sigh and a quick image of Willa races through my mind. I tagged along with her for summer band practice. She was a majorette who twirled her baton as if her life depended on it. When Mama didn't feel like taking her to practice, Aunt Mavis brought us her homemade butterscotch ice cream sandwiches and dropped us off at the football field. I stood in awe of Willa and the other majorettes as they perfected dance routines with the band's accompaniment.

"Aunt Mavis, let's take a spin downtown."

She heads toward the courthouse. We round the square and my heart skips several beats. To the right of the courthouse sits the same gas station Daddy and Uncle Ray frequented for oil changes and tires.

"Chamblee's is still standing."

"Always went toe-to-toe with Rachel's. The store is under new management now." Aunt Mavis chuckles and points at the competition.

We swing a left and the Drummer's Home stands tall and proud. This was Mama's home briefly, before she went to Georgia Mental. Clay sat at his cherry roll-top desk and wrote out checks for her rent on the twenty-eighth of each month for almost a year. She'd write me letters from the Drummer's Home and I'd refused to open them. He'd offered to read them, but I thought it best they be returned. The roller-coaster ride with her was too high and too frightening.

Aunt Mavis slows her pace so I can take in the city. I ache for the missing staples that have disappeared. Allied Department Store is gone, the place Mama stocked up on hosiery and bras. Deraney's was Willa's favorite store because the proprietor set aside Jordache jeans for her and allowed her to pay for them with her Captain D's earnings.

I look to the right and gasp. "What happened to the Hargrove Theater?"

"Burned down years ago. I was hoping they'd rebuild it. I loved double-dating with your parents there."

"Remember the Thanksgiving movie festival every year? Or the time Mama snatched the wig off that woman's head she thought Daddy was seeing?"

"All Paul did was fix Cathy Jean's bathroom cabinets, but your mother wasn't convinced."

Laughter fills the car and Whiplash releases a low growl as if she remembers the snatching too.

She taps the steering wheel. "We need to stop at IGA for Sure-Jell. Before you called, Ray and I were canning jelly and cucumbers. The kitchen is a mess. You've been warned."

She parks at IGA and fishes in her purse for money. I stop her frantic search.

"I've got a little over one hundred dollars," I joke.

"I beg your pardon?"

"Lamonte went to the bank—never mind. I'll get what you need."

My attempt at humor reminds me of how much I never knew him. I look at Aunt Mavis and decide to keep his funds siphoning to myself. She looks exhausted. Guilt fills me for having her come to my rescue.

"Tell me how many boxes I need to get."

"Get three of the small ones and Morton's Kosher salt." She hands me a twenty and I give it back.

"Your money's no good here."

Whiplash barks and scratches at the door.

"I'll be right back, girl. Stay put."

I head inside and am greeted with hellos and smiles. Lamonte promised me that when we retired, we'd move to a small town and purchase a gigantic house in the country with a wraparound porch.

I shake away that memory as I stop at the tomatoes. "Lamonte is no more. Lamonte is no more."

"Did you say something, Sugar?" an older man standing in produce asks me. He steps closer and I admire his blue linen leisure suit. He tinkers with the black-and-silver Medic-Alert bracelet on his left wrist and smiles, releasing a fresh burst of Listerine.

"I said tomatoes galore, tomatoes galore."

"They sure are pretty this time of the year. You can make some real good chow-chow with these green ones." He lifts one for me to inspect, then places the tomato with the others and extends his right hand. "Name's Battle. You from around here?"

"I'm just running in for my Aunt Mavis."

"Lawton?"

"Yes, sir."

"That's your aunt?"

I nod.

"I been knowing May and Ray for years. They're good people." He considers my branch on the family tree and touches my shoulder. "How your Mama and 'nem doing? Been a while since I've seen Greta."

"Everybody's fine." I swallow hard and do what I do best. "I am on my way to see her today."

"Tell her Battle said hey for me, okay? Me and Ray go way back. Fought in 'Nam together and everything. I knew he was gonna be something in the military. He always did have good leadership abilities. Your daddy, Paul, made the best cabinets in the South. Had the market cornered 'til he moved up North. Matter of fact, tell 'em all I said hello."

"I will, sir. Thank you for your kind words."

"You ain't got to be so formal. Call me Battle."

"Okay…Battle. I'll tell them you said hello."

I slink away in hopes no one else stops me for small talk. I could do this all day. This is what I longed for in Atlanta—a place to call home where someone knew me, knew my people. I make it past the honeybuns and breads and my stomach growls. I stop at the sound of raucous laughter between women one aisle over. As soon as I find the Sure-Jell, I will creep behind them to find the source of their joy.

"It's like I said, Norma, you can't beat good home training. These young folks don't know a *thank you* from a *please*. Forget about *ma'am* and *excuse me*. I don't know who's raising them, but that's been lost in the school system."

"Mmm-hmmm. Sure is."

I nod my amen and think of some of the youth I encountered while mentoring.

"When I was teaching, there was a respect code the kids had to follow. None of this sagging pants and earbud, head-bopping mess I see now. I don't know how these young teachers do it. I would have been on the news for slapping the taste out of their mouths."

"Shirley, quit. You have more tact and couth than that."

"Norma, did you hear who the cat dragged back into town?"

"Shirley, I've got to get my commodities and watch my stories. Make it quick."

"That ole' prodigal daughter of Greta and Paul's."

"Hush yo mouth!"

My legs are driftwood. I stay on my aisle, but inch closer to the bottles of salad dressing.

"You didn't see the story in the *AJC*?"

"Girl, no."

"You taking this unplugging from society too seriously. You know that girl left here years ago and nobody had seen hide nor hair of her until they did a story on the state of mental health in Georgia. But I knew where she was because of the lowdown way she did my granddaughter, Annette."

"Where was she all that time?"

"Up in Atlanta with Clayton."

"Myles?"

"Mmm-hmmm. I still can't look his ex-wife, Lorene, in her face. Looks like she would have known he was sweeter than a pecan pie, but she spent all those years holding on for nothing."

"Well, he is what he is. I'd rather he be himself than to pretend to want that woman and play with her feelings."

"Norma Ann Jasper, you've lost your religion! Ain't *nothing* right about what you're saying!"

I race to the next aisle and confront the women. "If you have something to say about me or my family, say it to my face."

Norma is the weaker one. She breaks their semi-circle, drops her face, and allows me enough space to face the bully, Shirley. Shirley slings her purse over her shoulder and tightens her grip on the handle in case she decides to swing it my way.

"I'm not changing one word. You should be ashamed to show your face around here. Pretending your mother is dead and acting like you don't have family in this town."

"Shirley, don't." Norma digs her fingers into Shirley's arm, but she is stronger than a planted tree.

Her voice grows louder. "It ain't like Atlanta is Los Angeles. Bet you were so proud of yourself sitting up on TV during that interview, showing pictures of you and your sister, like nobody knew who you were."

"What my family does is none of your business."

A small crowd gathers as Shirley gains momentum. "It is my business when my granddaughter speaks to you while taking her class on a field trip and you act like you don't know her!"

Her granddaughter, also my fourth-grade classmate, Annette Cousins, spotted me at the World of Coca-Cola. Her students gathered around her as she handed them tickets. I heard my name, but ignored it because I was taking a break to clear my head from a hectic project.

Her voice grew louder as I walked in the opposite direction. "Aren't you Antoinette Willamson from Sparta? We went to school together years ago."

She stopped me and I faced her. "You have me mistaken for someone else."

"It has to be you. I'd know you anywhere. Remember, the Hollywood Daddy game? Our shared bully, Lisa." She laughed but regained her composure when I wouldn't travel down memory lane with her.

"Truly, I'm not the person you're looking for. Sorry." I walked away with a ton of remorse.

Karma kicks in again as Shirley keeps going. "All she wanted to do was introduce you to her students since you'd done so well for yourself. She was so proud of her *successful* classmate." Her air quotes as she says *successful* are hard and vicious.

The crowd parts like the Red Sea as my aunt, uncle, and Whiplash approach us. "What's going on here?"

Shirley shifts her purse to the opposite shoulder. "Well, if it isn't Queen Mavis, the Sparta Secret Keeper."

"What did you say to her, Shirley?"

"Only that she's ungrateful and should be ashamed to show her face around here. Everything else she needs to know, you should tell her. Then again, that's not the Lawton way, is it?"

A few *mmmm-hmmms* and *ain't that the truths* fill the aisle. Aunt Mavis turns on her heels and I attempt to follow her out.

A familiar woman in the crowd in a stylish suit shoves a piece of paper in my right hand and lifts her fingers to her ear. "Call me."

Chapter 11

Greta

I should have never spoken to the paper. It's been a few days and Toni hasn't come to see me yet. I had this dream that she would run to the Cooper Building, demand to see me, then take me out to the courtyard and sit and talk with me like old times. I didn't expect Willa to come, but Toni…I wanted her to come to my rescue.

I've been going back and forth to the window, looking down. I don't know what kind of car she drives, but I'd know her if I saw her. She'll stop at Kroger on 441 and get me this big bouquet of pink, red, and blue flowers. Maybe she'll remember our Thursday night fish fries and stop over at James Fish and Chicken and get a dinner for me. Even though I haven't eaten in a few days, I would eat for her. I received an injection because they said I hit Annalease. I would never harm her.

'Halia is mad at me and hasn't been to see me. Jesus either. Clark is as irregular as a menopausal woman's period, so I don't think he's coming back. I'm a little disappointed in 'Halia. Maybe she's disappointed in me. I'm thinking back to the last time I saw her and can't figure out what I did wrong. We talked about our marriages, about her singing, and how she fed people in her neighborhood. Then we got into an argument about child-rearing. 'Halia said I should love both my daughters the same. She shook her head and folded her arms when I told her about Willa poisoning me. She said daughters didn't do such terrible things to their mothers and I should apologize.

I told her I would do no such thing. I knew what I was talking about and she didn't have a right to judge me. I shouted at her and told her just because she played concert halls and sang to large crowds didn't mean she knew about motherhood. Our argument was so bad Annalease stepped in to keep me from fighting with 'Halia. That's when they say I hit Annalease and knocked her unconscious. Now, she's been moved to another room. Nurse Whipple said she wanted to be by herself. I don't believe her because Annalease is like my third daughter. She hasn't been in the dining room for a few days and I wonder where she is.

Everybody is being taken away from me. I can't even get up to look out the window 'cause I'm woozy. I try to turn sideways and almost succeed before Nurse Whipple's chipper ass comes through the door carrying a tray of food and something to drink. It is humanly impossible for a person to be that happy all the time. She's got another thing coming if she thinks I'm eating today. She's all smiles, as happy as the smiley face scrubs she's wearing. The words *Put on a happy face* surround the smiles.

"Good afternoon, Greta." She says it like she's singing a show tune.

"What's so good about it?"

"You're alive and well! I can't think of anything better than that, Greta." She grins and I notice a plastic medicine cup on the food tray. I'm not eating the food, and I'm not taking those pills. If she tries to force them on me, I'll bite her.

"I brought pimento cheese sandwiches and sweet tea."

"I'm not hungry."

"You haven't eaten in days. Daniel told me you attacked him when he brought food on Sunday."

"I don't like him."

"He was doing his job. We're all concerned about you. I bet if you take your medication you'll feel so much better."

"I don't like taking meds."

"The sooner you eat and take your meds, the sooner you'll feel better. You'll be able to leave this room."

"Has my daughter come to see me yet?"

Nurse Whipple's smile glows brighter. "Not yet, but I believe she'll come to see you soon."

"You don't think she's mad at me?"

"Why would she be?"

"She hasn't been here and I want to know she's okay."

Nurse Whipple bends next to my chair. "I don't know about your daughter, but I promise Mahalia will come to see you if you eat."

"You know about 'Halia?"

"Yes. She said she can't come back around if your tummy's empty. She has to be able to have a conversation with you. Laugh and talk. How's she supposed to do that if you won't eat? She told me herself."

"Did she?" Whipple nods. "Did she say anything else?"

"She said you always eat pimento cheese sandwiches with her and she wants you to have one today."

'Halia knows me and what I like to eat. Whipple wouldn't know that unless 'Halia told her.

"If I guarantee Mahalia will visit, do you promise to eat?"

I nod.

She places the tray on the table near my bed. "May I eat my sandwiches first, then take my medicine?"

"Absolutely. You need something on your stomach before you take your pills anyway."

"Do you want one of my sandwiches?"

"Do I look like I need to eat another morsel?"

"No, you don't. But being big-boned suits you, Nurse Whipple. You have a nice size."

The sandwiches smell so good I wish she'd brought me three. I swig the sweet tea and take a bite of a sandwich. I wolf the first one down in less than two minutes. Either I'm hungry or this is the best food I've had in a while. Nurse Whipple passes me a few napkins and I wipe my mouth. I look around the room, hoping 'Halia is pleased enough to come sit with me. I'm so excited I wear myself out. I lean back in the chair and take my time with the second sandwich. The slower I chew, the dizzier I feel.

Restless days catch up to me when I'm tired. Nurse Whipple asks me to stand. She takes off my shoes and helps me into bed. She doesn't harass me about taking the meds as she takes the tray. I get comfortable in my fetal crook, turning my back to the door so 'Halia can tap my shoulder when she comes in. 'Halia can't see me with my back turned, so I face the door again. If I'm facing forward, she can come in and sing me a tune. Through a fog, I see Nurse Whipple backing out the door and smiling at me.

Chapter 12

"The nurse said the liquid Depakote worked," Uncle Raymond tells Aunt Mavis. "They put it in her sweet tea since she wouldn't take the pills."

She tilts her head back on the sunroom sofa and drinks another Bloody Mary. A phone call on the way home from IGA interrupted our inevitable Come-to-Jesus about Shirley's accusations. Before I could ask about the Sparta Secret Keeper label, a nurse asked Aunt Mavis's permission to put medicine in Mama's food. I had no idea she had an impact on her care or medication. I'm filled with more questions now and watch as Uncle Raymond sits next to her. He rubs her hands and shoulders. I scan the front lawn and watch as Whiplash drinks water from her bowl and chases butterflies.

"May, do you think it will be a good idea to bring her home again?"

"Not until our next meeting. I'm a bit more comfortable with the Depakote. I was worried about the long-term effect the Chlozaril might be having. That was constant bloodwork monitoring. I hated suggesting putting liquid in her tea, but after she attacked her roommate, I didn't know what else to do."

"She attacked her roommate?" I ask.

Uncle Raymond says, "Her hallucinations are growing wilder and she is angry the gospel singer, Mahalia Jackson, isn't coming to see her."

"Mahalia Jackson? She's been dead for years."

"Jesus has been dead longer, but she thinks He visits her, too," Aunt Mavis adds.

"What else does she do?"

They look at each other and Uncle Raymond takes the lead. "Since your mother has been away, we've made the effort not to abandon her. We used to pick her up twice a month, then the visits dwindled to holidays because of her erratic behavior."

Aunt Mavis chimes in and finishes his recitation as she always does. "We are well connected with the Georgia Mental staff. A few of them were my coworkers from my days at Oconee Regional. I made an unofficial pact with them to keep me posted on her care."

He places his fingers on Aunt Mavis's lips and redirects his focus to me. "Toni, I understand your anger about what we did, but you and your sister were in no position to help your mother."

"What about now?"

Aunt Mavis changes her position on the sofa. "What do you mean, now?"

I'm back at the mall again when I was a little girl. Why didn't my guardian angel let me ride to the hospital? Why didn't I help Daddy when she wouldn't take her medication? Shirley is right; I should be ashamed to show my face in this town. But I'm here now.

"Why can't I care for her now? Let's face it, my contracts are drier than the Mojave and Giovanna is locked into her lease for a year. I can stay here and watch her. I have enough money saved to take a hiatus." A bell dings in my head. "I can even renovate the home house. I overheard Clay say the house was still in the family."

Uncle Raymond and Aunt Mavis face each other. Her eyes ask for his consent before she speaks. "It is. Your father thought it best to keep the house in the family. It was paid for, but he feared your mother would destroy it."

"So the two of you took that away from her like everything else?"

"We didn't take it away."

"May I go in and clean it so I'll have a place to take care of her?"

"You can't, Toni."

"Everything about this family comes with secrets and strings. Why can't I go in?"

"Your father's stipulation was that nothing be done to the house without you and Willa agreeing to changes. You can't replace a thing without her consent."

"You're kidding, right?"

Aunt Mavis exits the sunroom and Uncle Raymond grows antsier. She returns with an accordion file and places it on the coffee table. She rifles through several slots and produces a document that she slides to me. I look at the paperwork, anger filling me as I read. In 1989, these heathens, these relatives of mine, drew up a document giving Aunt Mavis the deed to the house. Our names are listed as well. My dad made sure to include verbiage tying me to Willa and forever locking us together as sisters in disgrace. I toss the document back to her and stand. I have to leave before I lose my cool and say something I can't take back.

Uncle Raymond stands as well. "Don't leave. I think this is a good thing. This is a chance to reconnect with your sister. She'd be more than understanding about the matter."

"I agree," Aunt Mavis says.

"We haven't spoken in over twenty years. She doesn't want to have anything to do with me!"

"Times change. People change. The least you can do is reach out to her."

"And say what? Hi, Sis, I haven't seen you since Moby Dick was a calf, but may I have your permission to go inside our old house, please and thank you very much!" The words tumble out quickly and without pause. I take a deep breath and steady myself.

Uncle Raymond takes me by the hand, motions for me to sit again. He rubs my back, his favorite gesture from my childhood when I had a toothache or ate too much candy or Girl Scout cookies during movie night.

"Your sister and her husband, Donald, stopped to see us last year on their way to Orlando. They were headed to their vacation and rewarding McKenna for her school achievements."

"McKenna?"

"Your niece." He continues. "She told us she'd been trying to reach you for years, but you returned her letters unopened. She said whenever she called Clayton's, you were either busy or asleep. She stopped trying over the years because she thought you didn't trust her."

"It's not that, Uncle Ray."

"What is it?"

Words are playing hide-and-seek in my throat. "May I please get some fresh air? I'm taking a drive to clear my head."

He hesitated and sighed. "Be careful."

I grab my keys and head out front. Whiplash notices and races alongside me, lapping at my legs.

"I'll be back soon, girl."

She barks and follows me to the car. I unlock my phone and see several text messages from my friend, Jordan. She's left two voice-mails as well. I scroll through my contacts to find Willa's number. Russ added her number to my contacts in the basement studio after wine and cheese one night. He made me promise to reach out to her and insisted that she spoke with him and Clay often about us seeing each other again. Whiplash is insistent on taking a ride with me, but luckily, Aunt Mavis rescues me and takes her back inside. I leave their yard, emotions swirling, hands trembling. I miss creating projects and going to work every day. I don't know what to do with myself, but something inside tells me this is what I need.

I drive in silence and head to my childhood home. Downtown Sparta greets me again as I think of Willa. Like a snake charmer's victim, I'm lulled into a parking space in front of Webster's Pharmacy. When Daddy first taught her to drive, he coaxed her to pick up Mama's medication at Webster's. We'd run to the back of the store for ice cream first. Butter pecan for me, chocolate for Willa. The wonderful woman who waited on us must have known about our troubles and about Mama's penchant for swallowing M&M's whole. One day, when Willa picked up Mama's Thorazine, the ice cream lady suggested we mix one or two of her pills with the M&M's. That way, she'd have a sweet treat and get well at the same time. To demonstrate, she waited for Willa to bring the meds to the back of the store, gave us a Ziploc bag of M&M's, and mixed the meds in. The orange-brown pills passed for M&M's with flying colors. Mama never knew the difference.

I press Willa's number, sit back, and practice what I'll say. I wait for her to answer. It goes straight to voicemail and I hang up. I try again, and after four rings, I hear my sister's voice on her message and tear up. It has the same, authoritative sound as I remember, but softer. Maybe marriage and motherhood changed it. When she says, "Please leave a message after the tone," I pause and say, "Willa, this is Toni. I'm staying at May and Ray's for a while. Please call me when you get this message."

I press "end" and exit the car in search of our ice cream lady. I don't remember her name, but I feel compelled to thank her for looking out for us. As I enter the store, I place my phone in my pocket and feel the slip of paper from the woman at IGA. I look at her number and wonder if she has the answers to the secrets.

Chapter 13

Three weeks have passed since I received the phone number. I stare at it and contemplate calling her. I haven't told Aunt Mavis about the exchange because it will increase her angst. After the showdown at IGA, she's been reserved and going overboard with canning. She tells me and Uncle Ray it's for the Pine Tree Festival booth, but I catch her deep in thought as she stirs tomatoes and peaches on the stove. Ball jars line the counter and the whole house smells like a farmer's market or a vegetarian restaurant. Stacked high in the corner are more Ball jars.

"Set that box of lids on the counter for me," she says.

I set the box of wide-mouth lids next to the lined jars. "Do you need my help with anything else?"

"I'm okay for now. Ray took Whiplash to be groomed, so I have the kitchen to myself." Aunt Mavis turns from the simmering pot. "We need to discuss putting you on the visitation list to see your mother."

We sit at the table. She rifles through a manila folder and I glimpse the lengthy writing of the blinding white paper she holds. The GMH letterhead, courtesy of the fluorescent bulbs in the chandelier dangling overhead, stands out prominently.

"Here is next month's treatment team meeting notice."

"What exactly is the meeting about?"

"Once a month, Ray and I drive over to meet with your mother's social worker, dietitian, doctor, and nurses to discuss her care and treatments. Even if we don't attend, we receive a notice regarding her progress and her needs."

"Will she be there?"

"Of course. She's a part of getting better. She's been complaining about her meds lately."

"Thorazine?"

She shakes her head vigorously. "That drug is yesterday. Feels like last century even. Since you and Willa went back and forth to Webster's for your mother, lots of drugs have been created to help schizophrenia. She responds best to Zyprexa, but when she's out of control, she's given meds to help her sleep. Many of the antipsychotic drugs you all knew aren't prescribed anymore."

Her medication was like another child. A plastic Piggly Wiggly bag housed the pills she hid underneath their bedroom armoire. We hid in her closet and peeked through the door slots as Daddy tapped his watch. She held up four fingers indicating the last medication time was four o'clock. He believed her lies at first and always changed into the outfits she'd splayed on the bed for him. Willa and I waited until he took her out for dinner or a walk and slithered underneath the armoire, sidestepping the mouse-trap she placed near the bag, and swiped it. Willa emptied the bottles on the floor and we picked them up, tossing them like circus jugglers. We flipped them up and down and the rattling of Thorazine, Triafon, and Moban made music. The bottles tumbled, and as they fell, we took turns having random bursts of conversation. We moved from subject to subject just like Mama.

"How do I help her with the meds and her other needs?"

"Slow down, Mustang Sally! You can't rush into things. Let's start with regular visitation. You can see your mother seven days a week up until nine at night. That's why I need to get you on the list. She can't come down to the visitation room to sit with you if you're not listed."

"Does she ever leave the facility? Other than coming to stay with you and Uncle Ray?"

"The facility has lots of community outings. They go to restaurants, shop, and play bingo. Staff monitors them closely, and we make sure she has adequate clothing and money to go on trips."

"Why do you help take care of her and Daddy has nothing to do with us?"

"I love your mother. I never referred to her as a sister-in-law; she was my sister-in-*love*. Paul couldn't handle the situation. Especially after her health deteriorated."

"But he still has two children." I wait a few seconds and ask, "When was the last time you heard from him?"

"Two months ago."

My heart palpitates. Ever since he left, I sought acceptance from men because he denied us. Daddy sent me a check for $15,000 for my high school graduation and a lovely card. No return address and a New York postmark. Checks followed for my college and grad school ceremonies. When I pressed Clay about the matter, he finally said Daddy wanted to love us from afar.

"What did he say?"

"His usual checking-in call."

"Did he ever remarry?"

"He said he never will. Doesn't want more children either."

In a recurring dream, Daddy stands on the side of the shore with a massive bouquet of yellow roses for Willa and me. Handsome as ever and dressed to the nines, he opens his arms and waits for us to run to him. The three of us stand there. We take in his fragrant cologne and tickle the cherry-shaped birthmark on his neck, a distinctive beauty spot that pales in comparison to his milky dark skin. He holds the flowers overhead as Willa and I jump to reach them, never matching his lofty height. We walk hand-in-hand to his car, and he takes us to a new home where he treats us like princesses.

"I find that hard to believe. Women were always throwing themselves at him."

"Yes, they certainly did." She laughs. "My brother could have been a serious ladies man, but he only had eyes for your mother."

His denial is painful and genetic. It runs deep in my blood too.

"Do you need my help with the tomatoes and peaches?"

"Are you still going to the library?"

"It's been a while since I've checked my emails. Maybe someone wants Mustang Sally to decorate or design a green, energy-efficient home for them."

"Toni, you can use the Internet here."

"I know. I want to get out and roam the town. Since the IGA incident, I've been holed up like a fugitive. I can't hide forever."

"Suit yourself." She looks at the stove and the Ball jars. "I've got more than enough work to keep me busy."

"What are you selling this year?"

"Peaches, tomatoes, pepper and fruit-flavored jellies, chow-chow, pickled cucumbers, and muscadine wine."

"You've got skills. I can't boil water."

"You could if you wanted to. I'll be happy to teach you." Aunt Mavis struggles to stand.

"You okay?"

"Arthur's trying to get me, but I won't let him."

I stare at her, waiting to reveal this strange man.

"Arthritis."

"On that note, I'm heading to the library. I'll be back soon."

I had set a bag next to the front door earlier for the day's excursion. Denial runs in my blood. So does lying. I wave to Aunt Mavis as I head out to the door to connect with the woman from IGA. If I'm lucky, she can help connect the dots I'm missing about my mother.

Chapter 14

I push back doubts as I sit in the Washington EMC parking lot. Lying to Aunt Mavis makes my flesh crawl. But years of lying left me feeling as if I didn't have a conscience. I stare at the phone number. After a few cars pass, I dial. She answers on the first ring.

"Hello, this is Antoinette Williamson."

"Toni?"

"How do you know me?"

"Chile, we're first cousins. I'm Edwina, your Uncle Grady's daughter."

"Grady?"

"Listen, I'm fixing Walter's lunch. Come on down and eat with us."

"Now?"

"Yeah. You still know the town, don't you?"

"I think so."

"Where are you?"

"EMC parking lot."

"Come out and make a right. We're on the Sandersville Highway. Keep to the right side of the road, past Rocky's and Ameris Bank. You gonna keep going past Galilee Baptist Church for about three miles. My house is the black-and-white one on the right with the John Deere mailbox. You can't miss it."

Either I'm in the Twilight Zone or I've been sheltered too long.

This is the first time I've heard of an Uncle Grady. I know Norlyza and Carrie Bell—Mama's sisters—live in Alabama. That's where Willa went to live. No one ever mentioned Grady, though. Edwina has piqued my curiosity. How many other unknown relatives are out there? Grandma Rose kept so many secrets, it's hard to tell. We were forbidden to visit her when I was small, and I never questioned why.

The heat is stifling as I drive along this road. The weatherman promised a slight breeze for today's forecast. He was misinformed. If this car were a thermostat, the heat would be on hell. The hot air is soothing, though. It quells the butterflies in my stomach. Who goes to a stranger's house for food? A woman who wants answers, that's who. During Shirley's rant at IGA, Edwina's face stood out in the crowd. Her concern caught my attention. Sassy, middle-aged, and wearing a dressy suit in the middle of the day, everything about her was regal. Her high cheekbones and wide-set eyes resembled our bloodline. I shook it off as a coincidence since everyone in a small town is usually related by blood or love.

In no time, I spot the John Deere mailbox and pull into the driveway. I travel down a small hill and onto a circular driveway. Déjà vu hits me. Something is familiar about this yard. I get out and two cats greet me with purrs. One is blacker than the ace of spades. Its shiny coat gleams in the sun. A tan cat totters on three legs toward me. I hope they don't have Whiplash's licking affinity.

The front door opens and Edwina says, "Midnight, Tic-Tac, go on around back."

I shield my eyes from the sun and look at the top of the steps of the huge porch. Midnight and Tic-Tac are excited to have a guest as well. They disobey her and park themselves alongside one of many yard planters made from old tires. The gold, purple and white spray-painted tires have been fashioned as teacups and house beautiful flowers that know love and nurturing. Ignoring them, she descends the steps and sweeps me in a hug. She looks me over and hugs me again.

"You look just like Greta! A little of Paul too."

"Thank you."

She looks over my shoulder. "Does Mavis know you're here?"

"No, ma'am."

"Good. What we have to talk about today is between the two of us."

Her hair is covered in a decorative floral silk scarf. It matches her capris and dark-blue T-shirt. The McCallister bloodline—my mother's side of the family—comes in full view. Women on Mama's side have facial moles and a small hole above their right ears. I stare a bit too long and she becomes self-conscious. She touches the scarf.

"I was pulling weeds this morning. I can't let these flowers get away from me."

"I wasn't looking at the flowers or your scarf. Looking at your face, it's obvious we're kin."

"Ain't that the truth? Come on in so you can meet Walt."

I follow her up five or six steps, marveling at the variety of flowers on the porch and in the yard. Her place is a green thumb paradise. The moment I step inside the entryway, my mouth waters. I smell liver and onions with gravy. Clay's liver was the best I'd ever tasted, but I enjoyed sampling variations in other kitchens.

"Walt, she's here."

Her husband rises from a recliner where he's watching the news and greets me. Stacks of photo albums fill the coffee table in front of him.

"It's so good to see you again, Ms. Toni. I hadn't seen you since you were a little girl."

He smiles, steps back a few paces, and gives me the once-over. His long-sleeved dress shirt and jeans seem out of place in this weather. He pulls on his suspender straps and says, "Let's eat before Edwina's liver gets cold. You haven't had liver and onions until you taste hers. Bathroom's down the hallway. You can wash up in there."

I head down the hallway, sneaking glances at family photos along the walls. They are mostly of Edwina and Walter, but a few of them are of relatives I've seen sporadically. I stop when I spot a photo of me, my sister, and parents. I lift it from the wall, pondering the family that used to be. The teal scenery captured us with huge grins. Daddy is next to Mama, and they both smile. Willa wears a red dress and four plaits pulled high and held together by block-shaped ponytail holders. Front teeth missing, she protects me with her hands on my left shoulder. My dress is white and my hair is cornrowed in "the Peaches," thanks to the nurse's aide Aunt Mavis paid. I lift the velvet and cardboard backing from the frame and read the inscription: *The Williamson Family, 1979.* I place the photo back on the wall.

After washing up, I join them in the dining room. Walter says grace and Edwina starts our conversation over clanking silverware.

"I'm sorry about the article, but I'm glad you're home."

"I never meant to hurt anyone in the family."

"The McCallisters, our maternal relatives, don't do so well with mental illness. I guess we're like everyone else. But when we ignore a person, we ignore a person. I want the trend to stop with you and Willa."

She looks out the window and her husband picks up the conversation. "Far as I know, a few of the folks on Greta's side tried to help her, Edwina included, but the sicker your mother got, the stronger Mavis's grip tightened. We don't know what it was all about, but the next thing we knew, she was in Georgia Mental."

Edwina's side view solves the mystery. Her eyeglass chain takes me back to the mall meltdown. "It was you, wasn't it?"

She faces me. "Come again?"

"In the mall. Years ago at Hatcher Square. You were the woman who sat with me when they took Mama away."

"I sure did. I would have brought you home if Mavis hadn't stopped me. You asked me to call her, but I wanted to take you by the hand and bring you here with us."

"Why didn't I remember you or know we were related?"

"Greta started going downhill a little after you were born. We used to visit one another's houses all the time. All that acreage out in the country was the perfect spot for parties and picnics. But something happened one day at the Fourth of July cookout that changed everything. After that day, it's like you all fell from the face of the earth."

I stop chewing and give her my undivided attention.

"The children were bobbing for apples, your uncles and guys from the neighborhood were standing around the oak tree in the yard drinking beer, and your aunts and a few of our lady friends sat at the oblong table Greta put out for parties. She kept swatting at flies, or so we thought. She eyed us like we were stepchildren as we played spades. She shook her head, ran in the house, and came back with a shotgun."

I cough and drink tea as her story intensifies.

"She pointed that double-barrel straight at your Cousin Francine and told her to give back the gold coins she stole. Said the voices told her Francine had snuck in the window the night before and took the gold coins she had stashed in a flour tin."

"What did Francine do?"

"She tried to remain calm, but we could all see she was scared half to death. The men, including your Daddy, ran to the table from the oak. The children toppled the barrel of apples and ran for cover under the house. Your Daddy talked to Greta like he was talking fire out of a wound, telling her he had the gold coins and it was all a misunderstanding. We knew there were no gold coins; the Williamsons were big on keeping their money in the bank. That's how they have all this land in Hancock County. Paul convinced her to give him the gun and he took her inside. It looked like a father leading his child."

"Did anyone say anything? Do anything?"

"Everyone went home in fear. I told Francine watching Greta was like watching my Daddy all over again."

"Uncle Grady, correct?"

"Yes. You probably never heard of my father, since there's an eighteen-year age difference between him and your mother. He clicked out before you were born. He died in a mental institution in Florida a few years ago."

"I wish I had known. I mean, about him."

"Clayton knew about Daddy's death. He and Russell sent a beautiful arrangement to the funeral."

Walter releases my hand and pats my back. Edwina holds up one finger and he stands, empty plate in hand, and goes to the kitchen. He returns with a bag across his shoulder.

"I'm going to see a man about a mule."

"Walter Crittenden, one more Hurston phrase."

They laugh in unison, leaving me in the dark.

She reaches for the book on the buffet. "Walter's headed to the library for a one o'clock meeting. It's our One Book, One City reading program. The library picks a yearly reading list to discuss. July's book is Zora Neale Hurston's *Their Eyes Were Watching God*."

"I got sixty acres."

"Walter!" He doubles back and kisses her cheek. She blushes and gives his butt a light tap. "Get on out of here, old man!"

He leaves and I wrestle with my vanishing appetite. The food is delicious, but the more I learn about my family, the less I want to eat.

"I can wrap your plate up, Toni."

"I'd love to eat it later. I'm a little overwhelmed right now."

She takes our plates and I go to the bathroom to wash my hands. When I return, she's nestled on the sofa, patting the cushion next to her. Several photo albums are open, and I grab the nearest one.

"Ready for your history lesson?"

I nod and settle back on the sofa. Hours pass and I learn about my grandmother, Rose, my uncle, Grady, and all the relatives who dropped them like hot coals when their illnesses progressed. I lift the plastic shield and gently release a picture of Grady and a woman hugged up next to him at a Trailways bus terminal. I flip the photo over and read the date: *May 31, 1969.*

"Where was this taken?"

"Macon, Georgia." Edwina holds the photo, then hugs it. "This is my parents' last photo before he lost his freedom."

I wait for her to explain. Her eyes are misty, but she plows forward.

"Daddy had gotten his master's degree and my mother was so excited about him moving us to Texas. She thought he was stressed out over getting his degree. She ignored his behavior—waking up in the middle of the night and walking around the house talking to himself—but things grew stranger. She hid his behavior from us until the trip. He boarded the bus, and hours later, she received a call in the middle of the night about his outburst. He'd made it as far as the Texas state line when he was put off the bus. He said God came up through the floor of the bus and told him to kill the driver. The other passengers fought him, and my mother went to pick him up. She was uneducated about the mental illness maze and had him institutionalized. First, he went to Georgia Mental. We'd go back and forth to see him, even brought him to Sparta a time or two, but he was never able to function on his own. Back then, they didn't have all the modern treatments and medicine they have now. He received electroshock therapy and was later moved to Seaborn Hospital down in Florida. That's where he died."

"Mama never said anything about him as far as I can remember."

"The onset of her illness started after you were born. That's when we all noticed small changes in her."

So I caused my mother's sickness? "What about my grandmother?"

"Grandma Rose, my father, and your mother are the three who suffered most. I think that's why Norlyza and Carrie Bell didn't have children. I also believe that's why they took your sister in, too. Probably thought they could help the family out since we were so scattered."

Keep acting up and they're gonna send you to Milledgeville was the playground taunt when I was in school. It wasn't until Mama's meltdown that I understood the threat. I drop my head. The photo albums are filled with rich stories, people who share my DNA, and I don't know them. Edwina lifts my chin with her soft hands until we face each other.

"What are you going to do about your mother?"

"There's a treatment meeting soon that I plan to attend. I want to bring her to the home-house soon. I won't burden Uncle May and Ray with our presence."

"I can help you out with her. The one thing I share with Mavis is a nursing background. Daddy's illness made me pursue this field. Trust me when I say you'll need a break from time to time. Taking care of your mother won't be a picnic in the park. You have to keep her occupied and she has to stay on top of her medicine. Otherwise, she'll be right back at GMH."

"What else should I do?"

"Indulge her hallucinations. If she says she sees something, go along. If she thinks you're calling her crazy, she may lash out."

I ponder her instructions, unsure if I'm cut out for this. "I'll keep you posted."

I stand, not wanting to take up another minute of Edwina's time. She stands with me.

"Do you want me to put your food in Tupperware?"

"Yes, please. I haven't eaten good liver, onions, and rice since Clayton cooked. I wish I knew how to cook good Southern staples."

"My doors are always open for cooking lessons. We're family. Don't be a stranger."

She packs the food and walks me out. Midnight and Tic-Tac, still relaxing by the flowers, jump up and follow me to the car.

"Cousin Edwina, do I want to know why Tic-Tac has three legs?"

Edwina kneels and pets Tic-Tac. "He climbed up in Walt's truck one day. Thought he'd explore the engine. Walt started the truck not knowing he was there, and well…" I touch my chest. "Wasn't Tic-Tac's fault. Walt retired from John Deere a few years ago. He drove back and forth to Augusta for years, so Tic-Tac wasn't used to seeing the truck around."

We hug each other again and I get in my car feeling empowered. Today was a good start to putting the missing pieces of my family puzzle together. As I drive out of her yard, my phone buzzes. My day just got luckier. It's Willa calling.

Chapter 15

I'm exploring my childhood home as I wait for Willa. Daddy dubbed it the home-house because he said wherever we went in the world, if we succeeded or failed, we could always come back home. When I spoke with Willa a few days ago, I couldn't get the question, *Will you come see me?* out of my mouth before she said yes. I apologized for snubbing her and begged her forgiveness.

May and Ray have outdone themselves. A passerby would never know the house is empty. The freshly mowed lawn is reminiscent of the old days. The striped technique is the one Daddy used when we were kids. I'd jump on the riding mower with him as he rode the acreage making straight lines, then going in the opposite direction. He said since he didn't have sons that would play major league baseball, the yard may as well look like a baseball field. Green thumbs are in our blood. Hanging flower baskets and urns fill the porch. Seasonal flowers line a bricked path that encloses the oak tree in the front yard. The tree enhances the house's view. Willa and I took turns helping Daddy paint the shutters of our white house. Mama said the house always had to be white, but we could choose shutter paint. Deep burgundy was the last color we chose. A fresh coat remains.

I run to the backyard to see what other memories have been preserved. The clothesline anchored by two wooden posts remains. Mama said clothes were better hand-washed, so most Saturdays, she enlisted Willa and me to boil water and pour it in a huge silver tub while she went to work on our clothes using a washing board and Aunt Mavis's handmade soap. Never mind the fact we had a spanking brand-new Maytag washer and dryer in the laundry room. Daddy reminded her of this one Saturday when he snatched the soap from her hand and waved the purchase receipt from Sears in her face. He called her country and backwards. She called him stupid and susceptible to germs and the conspiracy of the traitors who rigged the machines with poisonous dyes that would stain our clothes and kill us all. They compromised; she washed the clothes in the Maytag, but hung them on the line.

The homemade fish cleaning table stands. Every Thursday, we'd gather round the table, line it with parchment paper, and carry trays of perch, mullet, and catfish for her to clean. She didn't want us getting scales on our bodies or cutting ourselves, so she shooed us inside with Daddy to play records and dance. She was in her own world when she prepared our dinner.

I travel farther on our land in search of the old well. The steep well frightened us all. Except Mama. She'd dance around it, dropping the bucket in the shallow hole and drawing water for her flowers. Daddy cemented the well when he caught her climbing in after one of her tormentors.

It has stood the test of time, its wooden shelter still intact. I lift the water bucket from the wood covering the cemented top. The oily, rusted chains alongside the bucket are slick and it slips from my grasp like an eel. I stoop to pick up the warped bucket.

"Tell us how you cut him!" a voice says.

My hands shake and I deepen my voice. "I didn't cut him with no knife."

The voice is closer now, and my insides warm as she says, "Last night, you told me you cut the dude."

My mock bass is gravelly as I recite our favorite scene in *Trading*

Places. "It was with these, I cut him. I am a chain belt in Kung-Fu. Bruce Lee was my teacher. Watch this."

I whirl around, left hand forward, palm of my right hand near my left wrist. I shout perfect karate sounds like Eddie Murphy. My standing leg kick is whip-fast and Willa laughs at me. I can't make my butterfly karate pose with my arms suspended in the air, right leg lifted, before we sweep each other up in a hug. I inhale the flowery smell of my sister's perfume, the fruity shampoo in her hair. She stands back so we can take a good look at each other. We each get an eyeful of twenty-three years of change.

"Little Sis! Antoinette Maria Willamson. Look at you!"

I'm underdressed compared to her. Golden brown and statuesque, she sports jeans and a classy Casual Friday blouse.

"Willadean Amber Willi—I mean Alston."

"My name is Willa. Dropped the Dean before I got shipped out of Sparta, remember?"

"You'll always be Willadean to me."

A moment of awkwardness passes between us before she takes my hand. "Come with me. I want you to meet someone."

We walk to her car, surveying the land of our youth. A smirk is the first thing I see on McKenna's face. When she sees us, she drops her head. Willa motions for her to speak, but she turns her back.

"McKenna, get out of the car. I want you to meet your aunt."

She huffs and exits the car, attitude for days.

"Hi." She thrusts her left hand forward and shakes my hand with as much enthusiasm as a taxpayer waiting for an audit. She glances at her watch and addresses Willa. "Mom, I thought we were here for a little while. I have a date with Uriah tonight."

"We'll be here as long as I say so."

"Mom, we're in the middle of nowhere!" She rolls her eyes at Willa and snorts.

Willa blows out a quick burst of air and says to me, "Give me a few seconds."

She points to the garden hose on the side of the house and they walk toward it. I don't know what Willa is saying, but her left hand is on her hip as her right fingers swirl in McKenna's face. McKenna's attitude disappears with each swirl. McKenna takes a deep breath, twists the ends of her curls, and heads toward me, Willa in tow.

My niece addresses me. "I'm sorry for my attitude."

Willa clucks her tongue and looks just like Mama when she says, "Aliens invaded her body six months ago. Maybe my teen will return before her eighteenth birthday." She asks McKenna, "Shall we try it again?"

"Hello, Aunt Antoinette. It's nice to meet you."

"Call me Toni. You can even drop the Aunt."

"Nice to meet you, Toni." The aliens have fled McKenna's body for the moment and she shyly asks Willa, "Mom, may I call Uriah?"

"Make it fast. We're going in the house."

Willa joins me and I give her an extra key to the house, courtesy of Aunt Mavis. "All these years, I thought the house was gone. It looks like somebody still lives here."

"Get this, Willa. Daddy's maintained the property all these years for the two of us. May and Ray have a cleaning lady who comes in twice a month to dust and sweep, and a company does a quarterly deep clean. He was afraid Mama would destroy the house."

"I'd have to agree."

"Willa!"

"Face it, you were her favorite. Her little gumdrop. She didn't give a damn about me and the feeling was mutual."

I slip the key in the lock, preferring to have this conversation inside.

I step inside the foyer and I see yesterday. Everything is the same.

From the scalloped mirror above the cherrywood table Daddy carved to a bowl of Aunt Mavis's homemade potpourri, the familiarity almost makes me forget the bad times.

Willa covers her mouth. "Look at him!"

We look at Mr. Juggles, the ceramic clown cookie jar on the table. Mama stuffed him with fortunes after double-dates to their favorite Chinese restaurant with May and Ray. For kicks, Daddy used to remove his head and place it on Willa's chest before she woke up on Saturday morning. He loved getting a rise out of her since she thought Mr. Juggles's head was creepy.

Willa lifts his head and pulls a fortune out. "You will do well to expand your business."

"I need that to come true yesterday. I'm afraid to check emails. I may as well sell Williamson Designs."

"This will blow over soon." She pulls another fortune from Mr. Juggles. "A person of words and not deeds is like a garden full of weeds."

"Is Lamonte's picture on that slip of paper?" I ask.

"You have to tell me about him."

"My lips are sealed right now. You don't want to hear all that cursing."

"Mama's precious little gumdrop doesn't curse."

Willa fishes around in the fortunes. "When we left for school each morning, I always hoped to pull out one that said, *Your mother's mental illness will be cured in three months.*"

She grows melancholy. McKenna joins us and Willa's face softens. "Mom, Uriah said hello. I didn't realize he was working tonight."

"See. All that attitude for nothing."

"I'm going back outside, Mom."

"No, check out the house with me and your aunt."

I grab Willa's arm and McKenna trails us. "Let's check out the place. I want to see if I need to modernize anything before I bring Mama home."

Willa stops near the dining room. "You're bringing her here?"

"If the hospital will let us. She wants to see us."

"I won't stop you from bringing her home, but I don't want to see her."

"Please reconsider. She misses us."

Willa waves off my request and heads to our old bedroom. McKenna and I follow her. She opens the closet door and pulls out an item housed in a black dry cleaning bag. "Did Mavis clean this?"

I shrug, unsure of who's done what over the years. She unzips the bag, revealing her majorette uniform. She removes the gold and maroon outfit, still sparkling. A pair of gold gloves and hat complete the set.

"What is that?" McKenna asks.

"My majorette uniform."

'You were a majorette?" McKenna touches the outfit. She is in awe her mother had a life before she came along. "I guess I got my dancing skills from you. Wait till I tell Uriah." She breaks into a dancing routine for us.

When she's done, I say, "It is in your genes. I got skipped on the dancing skills."

McKenna places her extra appendage, her cell phone, to her ear and leaves us alone. We kick off our shoes, collapse in our childhood bed, and catch up on old times.

"Strange reunion, but I'll take it," I say.

"I hated you for so long. That may even be an understatement about my feelings toward you. I couldn't hold on to that anger, though. As I matured, I realized we both were victims of our circumstances." Willa pauses. "May I ask you something?"

"Anything."

"Why did you return my letters? Why did't you answer my calls?"

"I wanted to forget everything. One lie turned into two. Two became twenty. After a while, I couldn't stop them."

"Couldn't or didn't?"

"Didn't."

"I took it personally and it hurt."

"You shouldn't have. Russ and Clay encouraged me to keep in touch, but I was so confused about everything."

"Aunt Norlyza said the same thing."

"What?"

"For as messed up as our family is, she wouldn't keep in touch either. Said we'd be lucky to see each other again. When a McCallister vanishes, they Bermuda Triangle-disappear."

"Did you know about Uncle Grady?"

She nods. "I learned about Grady and all the other cousins and siblings who had no help or support services years ago." She looks out the window. The well is in full view from our room.

"What are you thinking?"

"I wished Mama would have fallen in the well. Or left us for another man. Her illness cost us so much."

"I know."

"I didn't make friends until I moved to Alabama. Everyone here knew about our situation and shunned us."

"Same here. Well, my situation was a little different because of my living arrangements with Russ and Clay. I'm not sure which was worse: being shunned because of your crazy mother or your gay guardians. It's amazing when people show their true colors. "

I retrieve my phone and check texts. Of the three I have, two are from Jordan. I slip it back in my pocket.

"Aunt Mavis told me about your engagement party. I'm sorry."

"Not half as sorry as I am. All that money I wasted on good food, too." My attempt to ease my embarrassment fails.

Willa takes my hand. "It takes time to get over a relationship. How long did you date?"

"Five years."

"That's epic. People don't stay married that long."

"Speaking of marriage, how long have you and Donald been married?"

"Seventeen years."

"That's epic," I say, imitating her voice.

"We've had our ups and downs, but I told him about our family the moment we got closer when we were UAB freshmen. I'd lived with too many lies."

"And he accepted everything?"

"We had more in common than we knew. He has a few family members in the same predicament. His family is more open about it than ours."

"Willadean the Brave."

"Willa Alston, thank you very much! Gumdrop, if it's any consolation, I saw Lamonte's photo in the *Atlanta Business Chronicle*, and you should be happy he broke things off with you. That big-head man would have ruined my nieces' and nephews' heads!" She pretends to blow a balloon and rotates an invisible globe with her hands.

"Only nephews. The Dunlaps are boy breeders."

Willa winces at the thought and asks, "When are you going back to Atlanta?"

"In a week or so. I have to handle some business and transfer some money from my account in Atlanta to here. I know I can do a wire transfer, but I have to stop at Russ and Clay's. Russ took some time off from studio work and traveling to take care of Clay at the house."

"I'd love to see them again."

"Our *casa* is *su casa*. I'm sure they won't mind if you stop in. They are the only folks I know who don't mind unannounced visits."

"I'll stop by."

We keep chatting as two hours disappear. I speak with her husband, Donald, who invites me to come and see them when time permits.

Willa slides off the bed and slips her shoes on. "I've got to get back to Birmingham. We have church in the morning." She hugs me and caresses my chin. "Don't apologize anymore. I never blamed you for being distant. I only wanted you to realize we were in this together."

Tears well up and I fear that if she leaves, I won't see her again.

"Don't cry. You have a big sister again, and you're not getting rid of me."

I link arms with my sister and walk with her outside. McKenna chatters away on her phone in the front seat as Willa gets in. We wave to each other as she backs out of the driveway.

Inside again, I lift Mr. Juggles's head and swipe a fortune. "Forgiveness doesn't change the past, but it does enlarge the future."

Chapter 16

Greta

"I have a surprise for you," Nurse Whipple says.

Annalease sits on the floor in front of my bed. I part her thick hair and grease her scalp as gently as I can as a peace offering for hitting her. She munches on Puffcorn as I ask her to face the window.

"Surprise for me?"

"I'm not supposed to say anything, but you've been so good taking your medicine the last few weeks."

"My treatment meeting is coming up."

"That's not the only reason you're taking your meds, is it?"

"I want to get better."

I wait for 'Halia to pat me on my shoulder, but she doesn't. Neither Jesus nor Clark speaks. The more I take my medicine, the more I feel like the old me. Last week, I dreamt I was back in the classroom teaching. I'll ask Mavis to help me get my teaching license renewed. The requirements are probably different now.

"Take your Zyprexa so I can share the good news."

I tie the end of Annalease's braid with a pink rubberband and take the white cup from Whipple. Annalease turns around to see if I'll put the medicine under my tongue. I swallow it with pride and give the white cup back to her.

"Guess who was added to your visitation list?"

I can't contain my joy. "Toni?"

Whipple claps her hands together like she just won a stuffed bear at the Georgia State Fair. "Yes! She was added this morning. I'm sure she'll attend the treatment meeting next week."

I haven't had news this good since 'Halia told me I wasn't a marriage failure.

"Are you sure, Nurse Whipple?"

"Would I lie to you?"

"As far as I know you wouldn't."

Annalease's shoulders bunch. She jumps up from the floor, plunks hard on her bed, and pulls her knees to her chest. She rocks a little while before tears stream. "I thought I was your daughter."

Nurse Whipple intervenes, smiling like she always does. "Annalease, you're all her daughters. There is so much love in the world to go around. You wouldn't want Greta to keep it all to herself, would you?" Annalease shakes her head. "Just think of having two other sisters. An extended family, if you will."

I guess I am all the family Annalease has in the world. She came to GMH five years ago. She stabbed her grandmother forty-five times because she wouldn't sign a permission slip for a Washington, D.C. school trip. From what I read in the paper and what I heard the others whispering about, outpatient mental therapy in her hometown of Dublin, GA, would have helped Annalease, but the family was too ashamed to get treatment. Before she snapped, she bounced around from house to house until her grandmother took her in. A social worker helped her grandmother obtain a disability check since Annalease was underage. At the time of the stabbing, she was eighteen. They didn't take her to YDC, the youth correctional facility, and she was too old to be placed in the youth building here. I took an interest in her after no one in her family would visit. She's been with me ever since.

I sit on her bed. "Annalease, I have three daughters, and you are my baby girl. How does that sound?"

She lifts her head and extends her legs. "You promise?"

"Pinkie promise."

She gets off the bed, picks up the box of rubber bands, and sits on the pillow on the floor again in front of my bed. I washed her hair after seeing her stained shirt collar and dandruff so big it looked like sawed wood flakes. I scratched as much of it as I could with the end of my rattail comb and made sure her hair was fresh and clean before I braided it. This is the same thing I used to do with Toni's hair.

If Whipple is right, there's a good chance Toni might take me home if I can prove myself worthy. I have to get my luggage out of the closet in case she picks me up. It's in the upper right side of the closet where Jesus placed it. He used to float in the closet and around the room keeping an eye on us. It wasn't my imagination, although Annalease has a different version of how it got up there.

I've been at GMH so long I've forgotten how to do some things everybody else takes for granted. Whew! I feel all sixty-two of my years as I relax my arms from doing Annalease's hair. I was thirty-nine when that little incident happened at the Hatcher Square Mall. Since then, being here has almost been like a sentence; Toni picking me up will be like my parole. I have to wait to go to the dining hall here. I can't just get up, go to the refrigerator, and taste strawberry yogurt on the gold spoon Paul gave me. I can't watch the spinning propeller on Jerry Wenn's crop duster like I did when I was out in society. I miss picking scuppernongs and making wine with Mavis.

"Good old bullets!" I say to Annalease, relishing the memory of wine on my tongue.

"We can't have a gun in here!" Annalease tenses.

"I'm talking about fruit, Annalease."

I calm her with a shoulder rub. Memories are rushing through my mind and I can't stop them. There was nothing like going to St. John's A.M.E. and dressing the girls up in their Sunday best. We sat in the living room and waited for Paul to put on his suit, fancy tie, and shiny cuff links. Pastor Wilcox, a few years ahead of me in school, became the pastor of the church after being appointed by the presiding elder. Before I came here, he and Sister Wilcox prayed with me and told me above all else, the Lord was all I needed.

I want to be out amongst people again. If I have to take medicine to do it, then so be it.

Annalease lifts the jar of Royal Crown grease as a reminder to come back to her hair. "Didn't you tell me Toni was getting married? You decided what you wearing to the wedding?"

"Mavis told me it's been called off."

"What for?"

"I'll let you know when I find out."

I loop a few more rubber bands on the ends of her braids and rest my hands and arms. These old fingers aren't what they used to be. Neither am I. I've been in and out of this place twenty-three years. Imagine spending your sixty-second birthday at a mental hospital. Whipple got me a caramel cake and raspberry fruit bars from Ryal's Bakery. The other residents sang "Happy Birthday" to me and I looked in their faces for Paul, Toni, Willa, Mavis, Raymond, anyone I knew who'd say this was all a bad dream and I'd be going home soon.

I want to sit on my porch again. I want to scrape the catch of the day from the old pond at my fish cleaning table. I want to laugh and talk with girlfriends like I see the ladies on TV doing. I want to be trusted. I want people to extend their hands to me in fellowship, not jerk away in fear. I'll negotiate my wants with Zyprexa. That's how I'll do it.

Chapter 17

I slip my key in the lock of Russ and Clay's house and steady the box of canned items from Aunt Mavis. I smell and hear evidence of summer cleaning. Russ doesn't believe in spring cleaning. His motto is if you do a little often, you don't have to break your back when spring arrives. He is the Felix to Clay's Oscar, the one who keeps things in tiptop shape. He taught me everything I know about being orderly. When I grew up in this house, Clay dashed out to the corner bistro on Saturday mornings when we cleaned and always told Russ, "Come get me when it's over." He made it sound like we were committing a crime.

"Hello, where is everybody?" I follow the sound of Tom Jones to the kitchen.

Clay's wheelchair sits in the middle of the living room floor, so he's either sleeping, or burying his hands in herbs from their garden. The afghan Mrs. Poole, our next-door neighbor, knitted for him is slung across the wheelchair along with a bag of honey-roasted peanuts. I look on the table and smile at the sight of a glass of Coca-Cola with a few nuts floating on top.

Russ is on his hands and knees, scrubbing the floor and singing "Lusty Lady." He shakes his head when he sees me, as if he has to get out the next lyrics. He points to me and I add, "That's all the paper said."

He gets up, shimmies, and steps in stride to the music as he takes the box from my arms. He continues to sing and puts the items on the table. He lowers the volume.

"They can keep blowing smoke up Robin Thicke's ass if they want to, but Tom Jones was the original blue-eyed soul man. Had the black women to prove it."

I ignore his comment. I'm not having an entertainment debate today. Especially about their icons, whom I only know of because of Russ's connections.

"Where is Clay?"

"Taking a nap."

"I'm going to check on him. Be back in a sec."

"I'll hurry with the floor. We have to talk to you about something."

Russ transformed our first-floor office to a bedroom after Clay got worse. Clay's time is divided between an assisted living facility and our house. He gets lonely, Russ comes off the road to his rescue. After Clay's illness progressed, it didn't make sense to go up and down the stairs for anything, so upstairs is virtually non-existent. I walk into the bedroom as Clay grapples with his oxygen mask. The tank is situated next to his bed, but he struggles to turn sideways.

"Let me help," I say, rushing to his side.

"Damn Tom Jones. I can't get a decent wink of sleep when Russ plays that God-awful music. Give me Marvin Gaye, Little Beaver, even. But Tom Jones? Humph!" He coughs and reclines on fluffed pillows. "I'm getting tired of hearing 'Lusty Lady,' all the time. If he wants to play the song, he should play Johnny Bristol's rendition." Clay scans the room and lowers his voice; this is his way of complimenting a handsome man out of Russ's earshot. "Bristol was a cool drink of water, let me tell you. That voice!" He fans himself, knocking his oxygen mask askew.

I readjust the mask. "Clay, you played Johnny Bristol's 'I Wouldn't

Change A Thing' over and over again when you got sad. I never asked you why."

"You remember that?" His weak voice evens out a bit.

"Of course. I didn't know what to do. You looked so sad, so lost."

"Damn, your memory is like an elephant's." He rubs his hands. "Hell, you're grown now. No need in hiding the truth. It was the only song that soothed me regarding the way I left Lorene. She was a good woman, but I couldn't lie to her or myself anymore. I needed to be free. Free for me is being with Russ."

"I see."

"I didn't care about the labels, the things people said about me. If you remember nothing else I tell you, Toni, chew on this. You'll know you've made the right choices in life when you come out on the other side of a decision and realize you'd do it all over again."

He is the weepiest man I know, so before he cries. I ask, "Do you need anything?"

"Bring my Coke and nuts, will you?"

I head back to the living room and he stops me with his faint voice. "Bring the wheelchair too."

I go back to the living room to pick up the items. I lift the Coke from Clay's hand-painted coaster and eye a stack of paperwork. NAMI Georgia. I want to pry, but shuffle the papers aside, fold the afghan, place it on back of the wheelchair and put the Coke in the cup holder. I head back to Clay's bedroom and hum Tom Jones in rebellion.

"Bring that chair as close to me as you can," Clay says.

This is when our game begins. As his body weakened, we'd recite a tune or rhyme to lessen the agony of getting him out of bed. He inches to the edge of the bed, takes in oxygen, and waits for me to lift him. His emaciated, splotchy face looks to me for a rhyme. He starts the show.

"This is the church."

I turn the chair sideways. "And this is the steeple." I sit his frail body upright and smooth my hand over tufts of his thin hair.

He leans forward so I can lift him. "Open the door." His watery eyes say it's okay to do a final lift.

"And see—"

"All the damn hypocrites who'll let me sing in the choir, put on their makeup, but send fire and brimstone down on me the minute I turn my back!" He interrupts me with a tongue-lashing as I place him in the wheelchair. He breathes into the mask and between puffs asks, "Was that a good one or what?"

"Next time, we'll do Mary Mack."

"I can make magic with Mary, too. No doubt."

I whirl the chair around at his request and push him into the living room. Russ is waiting for us with a tray of teacakes and fresh squeezed lemonade. Fear fills me. Aunt Mavis had said they wanted to speak to me, but wouldn't tell me why. Looking at Clay's appearance, I hope this isn't a goodbye visit. He's too young and feisty to die.

"What did Mavis tell you?" Russ asks.

"She said the two of you wanted to talk to me about something," I say, shifting my attention to Clay only.

Sensing my fear, he looks me square on and says, "Baby, I have a team of Alaskan Huskies pulling me in the Iditarod Race of Life. I ain't going nowhere soon." He makes his famous bang sign with an invisible gun and sips Coke through a straw.

"The reason we called you here is because..." Russ hesitates. "We're moving to Florida and we're closing the house. I'm not ready to sell it yet, because it holds so many great memories for us, but I'm sure you want to do something with your dolls and child-hood items."

I sigh.

"That's why Russ pulled me out of the assisted living facility. He's finally retiring from his music. The air down there will be better for my emphysema. I can sit near the beach and make him cook those good meals to fatten me back up." Clay looks at Russ and they smile at each other.

"Of course. I can move my things into my unit. I have plenty of room."

They look at each other and Clay tests the waters with a nod in my direction.

Russ winks and turns to me. "The other reason we called you here is because Mavis tells us you've been added to Greta's visitation list."

"I have."

"She also says you're thinking of bringing her home."

The temperature dips and goose bumps fill my arms. "I am."

Russ gathers the papers I saw earlier and hands them to me. "After the treatment team meeting and before you bring her home, reach out to NAMI."

"NAMI?"

"It's the National Alliance on Mental Illness. There is a Family-to-Family support group in Milledgeville. You'll need a support system to help you care for your mother."

I fling the papers on the table. "I don't need anyone to help me take care of my mother. I feel badly enough for being separated from her so long."

"That was for good reason," Clay adds.

"And the reason would be?"

He sucks on the oxygen mask and encourages Russ to continue the conversation with a hand swish.

"What we're trying to say, Toni, is after the honeymoon phase of being reunited with your mother wears off, you'll have to deal with day-to-day issues of caring for her."

"Aunt Mavis told me the team participants will help me with those things."

"The team may not be there when your mother stops taking her medication. Or when she decides *you* are poisoning her as she accused Willa of doing."

"My mother loves me. She would never accuse me of those things."

Clay coughs. He uses the handles of his chair to sit erect. "Toni, this is complex. Take the paperwork and at least read it."

I've trusted them for years, but no one knows my mother better than I do. If I can get her back to the house, to her old environment, she'll come around and be herself again. I pick up the papers from the table and clutch them.

"I'm going upstairs to check out my old bedroom."

I climb the stairs slowly, incensed at Russ and Clay's tag-team. My room is the same. Dolls line the bed. Michael Jackson, The Temptations, Prince, and the Time are a few of the artists whose posters are still affixed to the wall. I scan the room and remember the good and bad times I spent here. Early drawings are still rolled up and stacked neatly on my desk. This room birthed my desire to create buildings and monuments. Instead, I settled for interior design as a career choice. I pick up my Dream Skater doll, the one that made the journey from Sparta with me all those years ago. Mama went back and forth until she finally chose this doll. She picked this one out at Hatcher Square for my birthday the day she was taken away. I bet she'll be happy to see Dream Skater again.

Chapter 18

After dropping Whiplash off at Barkerfeller's, Aunt Mavis insists I drive to the treatment team meeting. "You need to know where you're going since you'll be visiting Greta," she says from the backseat.

I'm driving her and Uncle Raymond as they both sit in the back. Neither wanted to join me for a shotgun ride-along. I turn onto the grounds, and for a moment, I'm feeling lost.

"Are we going the right way?"

"You're doing well," Aunt Mavis says.

"It'll become second nature once you make the trip a few times," he says.

I take instructions from them and vaguely remember landmarks I pass. Uncle Raymond tells me the Hatcher Square Mall is now Milledgeville Mall. So many things have changed in the city since we visited here years ago. We make a sharp turn and I see a sign leading to GMH. As we approach the location, I'm stunned. The grounds look like a college campus. White stately buildings and a few dwellings that look like regular homes line the path I'm driving.

"Who lives in the homes?"

"Doctors," Aunt Mavis says.

"There are also dorms on the grounds for employees who don't want to drive home throughout the week," he adds.

I approach a speed bump and Aunt Mavis makes me stop. "Pull over there." She points from the backseat.

The three of us get out and face a hulking pecan tree. The tree sits across from an impressive, four-columned chapel that commands my attention.

"The chapel is beautiful," I tell them.

Uncle Raymond's voice grows solemn. "Your mother prays in there from time to time."

This revelation describes her to a tee. Church filled a lot of her time during our childhood. On the third Saturday of every month, Daddy and a few other men in the church mowed the lawn and cleaned the areas around the cemetery. Mama made Willa and me to clean the inside of the sanctuary. We'd sweep the floors, douse our rags with Murphy's oil, and polish the altar wood to a high gleam. We replaced the hymnals left on the velvety pews by Sunday parishioners and always left the sanctuary smelling like Pine-Sol.

Aunt Mavis grazes my arm. "This is your mother's favorite place on the grounds. When the pecans fall around October or November, she and Annalease come down with a few other residents and pick nuts."

Several people in scrubs walk the grounds and a few animals roam about on leashes with their owners. My stomach is in knots as we start our journey again to her building.

Uncle Raymond speaks to me as if I'm one of his soldiers. "Don't treat her differently."

"Act as if time hasn't passed, and if she says something unusual, which she will, go along with it," Aunt Mavis says.

Uncle Raymond points. "To the right. The Cooper building."

We park in front of her building and I take deep breaths before getting out. Mama's face is pressed against the front window as we walk up the steps. She points at me and I wave to her. A woman standing next to her leans into her ear and says something, and she steps away from the window. She runs to me once we're inside the building.

"I knew you would come, Toni. I knew you would come."

She holds me in a tight embrace and I gently release her strong hands from the rigid, boa constrictor-grip she's wrapped me in. I put her at arm's length and look at her. Time has been good to her. Her hair is still a mass of flowing curls and a few gray hairs kiss her temple. A semi-permanent rinse could remedy this look, since she said she never wanted to turn gray. Her skin is still taut and golden brown with a few moles. I turn her face sideways and see the McCallister ear hole. She wears black slacks, a mint-green silk blouse, and black polished Naturalizer clogs. The outfit is a throwback from her teaching days. Aunt Mavis said she rarely wore the jeans, T-shirts, and athletic shoes she'd brought to her throughout the years. A woman in smiley face scrubs introduces herself.

"I'm Anna Whipple. I'm Greta's charge nurse. Her doctor, dietitian, and social worker will also be present today. This meeting is two-fold, as we'll be discussing her treatment and preliminary discharge."

"Discharge?" Mama's eyes light up and she practically does a jig.

"Nothing's been finalized, Greta. We have to assess your support system and make our decision based on our findings." Anna knocks the wind from Mama's sails and her shoulders slouch.

Mama holds my hand as Anna guides us to a room on the first floor. The team members introduce themselves and Mama sidles next to me. Self-pity rears its ugly head. My eyes are immediately drawn to everyone's wedding rings as they sit at an oblong table in front of the room. For the first time, I notice Mama's wearing her anniversary gold band from Daddy. I trace the small Anhk symbols he had engraved on the ring. Inside the ring, he carved *G&P4EVER*. I whip out the notepad Aunt Mavis gave me and scribble Mama's progress as each team member speaks.

A woman at the far end of the table stands. "I'm Mara Groves, and I'm Mrs. Williamson's dietitian. She has eaten well this past month. With the exception of being fed in her room a few days, her appetite is healthy."

Mama whispers in my ear, "They fed me in my room after they say I hit Annalease."

I pat her hand to quiet her.

Aunt Mavis addresses her doctor. "Dr. Wells, has her lab work changed since stopping the Clozaril?"

"Yes. Switching her back to Zyprexa worked. The monthly labs were tedious and she didn't respond well to the medication."

She whispers in my ear again. "Felt like a woman stranded in the middle of the sea when I was on that medication."

"Shhhhh."

The roles have reversed and I'm uneasy. As she whispers in my ear, I feel as if I'm parenting her. I put two fingers on her lips to quiet her. She sucks in her lips and sulks.

"In a letter you wrote two weeks ago, you mentioned taking Mrs. Willamson home. As her power-of-attorney, what are your plans?" Dr. Wells asks Aunt Mavis.

She stands with confidence. "We've worked hard to ensure a safe haven for Greta in our hometown. Her daughter, Toni, has taken a leave of absence from her job to care for Greta, and we've reached out to several community organizations to make sure we engage her once she's out. Also, the probate court has designated Toni guardianship over Greta since she'll care for her daily needs. Her case manager has contacted us about accessing SSI."

"I don't want a check."

"Shhhh."

Aunt Mavis looks at Mama then continues. "We've ironed out all the details to ensure a smooth transition."

"Where will she stay?"

"In her house."

"Thought the house was gone."

"Be quiet, Mama."

I lock eyes with her social worker, Ethan, as he twists his wedding band. Damn, he's handsome. And fine. The electricity I feel right now requires a drink later tonight. I'm aching for Lamonte.

Ethan is everything I love in a man—tall, mysterious, and bald. I watched him stroll into the meeting, muscular and assured. When he introduced himself, I caught a whiff of Lamonte's cologne and almost swooned. His dark eyes cast a spell as we shook hands. It's been four months since the Blue Willow Inn debacle and four months since I've felt the touch of a man, experienced intimacy, or been close enough to a man to flirt. I miss it. Damnit, I miss it! I should be paying attention in this meeting, but I'm lusting after a stranger. Lamonte always complained about making love in the dark and never seeing my body. I had taken all the light bulbs from my lamps and ceiling in my bedroom so he would never see the full Monty. We were never intimate in the Conyers' house. I promised he'd see it all on our wedding night. So much for that dream.

"What social activities have you planned?" Ethan asks.

I shake off my lustful desires. "Bingo, shopping, and visits to Lake Sinclair. Mama can wet a hook like a man." Ethan's eyebrows shoot up. "She enjoys fishing."

He relaxes, gives a soft chuckle, and holds my gaze.

"Well now, this concludes the meeting," Nurse Whipple says. "When do you plan on picking your mother up, Toni?"

I eye today's date on my cell—October 15, 2007. "In two weeks."

"That should be fine. We'll have discharge papers ready when you arrive."

"May I come to the Pine Tree Festival?" Mama asks.

"I'll be here Monday after the festival. That's too many people and too much activity for you."

"I haven't been in years."

"Maybe next year. We'll see how things go this year."

After Nurse Whipple adjourns the meeting, May, Ray, Ms. Groves, and Dr. Wells stand in the hallway and chat. Ethan trails Mama and me. I assume he is leaving for the day until he says, "Toni, may I speak with you a moment?"

Flushed, I ask Mama to step aside. Nurse Whipple witnesses the exchange and takes Mama near a set of chairs in the lobby. Ethan directs me to a small corner on the opposite side of the building and leans against the wall as he speaks.

"It's wonderful meeting you face-to-face. I've worked with your mother the last four years, and you're all she talks about."

"Oh." *I was hoping you'd flirt with me.*

"My heart went out to you after the *AJC* article ran. I hope this is a new start for you and your mom. She has a scrapbook of articles about you she's collected over the years."

"I hope this is a fresh start as well. Thank you for all you've done for her. Aunt Mavis and Uncle Raymond are the only connections to family she's had over the years."

"I know. Every year at Christmas, they gift the Cooper residents with fruit and goodies. They are a godsend."

We stare and smile at each other a few moments. He looks at his watch. "Gotta run. My wife is at the hair salon for her standing appointment, and I have to pick the kids up from soccer and piano practice. Take care, Toni."

Mama and Anna come over again. I watch Ethan leave, longing for the day someone will have my back and love me for me.

Chapter 19

I awake in Aunt Mavis's house with Whiplash licking my face.
Why she hasn't bothered Willa or McKenna is a mystery. Maybe the tears, or the invitations strewn about on the bed, or the
half-nursed bottle of brandy I tossed in the corner is an indication
I need something. Someone.

I punch the pillow and turn on my side. Today would have been
my wedding day. I curl in bed in my pajamas and fondle my engagement ring. It's six in the morning. I'd crafted a handwritten message
on a scroll for Lamonte. My flower girl was to deliver the scroll
at four-twenty p.m., forty minutes before the ceremony. So many
tender moments were planned that I'll never see.

I have to pull myself together for the Pine Tree Festival. This
event is Sparta's homecoming. Residents from near and far fellowship and visit each other. They sample wares, signify, and talk about
how things used to be in their heyday. May and Ray's street team
will be in full force today. For the last three days and nights, we've
been labeling jars, assembling the floating pantry, and taking a
few preorders for sales. Donald, Willa, and McKenna arrived from
Birmingham last night, and we all went to dinner in Milledgeville
at Applebee's. Willa refused to visit Mama, and I didn't press the
matter.

A light tap on the door interrupts my pity-party. "Toni, breakfast is ready," Aunt Mavis says.

"I'm not hungry."

My back is still turned, but I hear a slight creak of the door. "You okay?"

I sit up and press my back into the pillows. Aunt Mavis's face is glowing and she holds a cup of coffee. Whiplash runs to her feet as she walks toward the bed.

"You sure you want to come to the festival?" she asks. "We can manage the booth if you want to stay here."

"It's the only thing to get my mind off the big day that will never be."

"Big day with Lamonte. There's another man out there for you. Mark my words."

"Not in this lifetime. Not that I want another man."

"You'll change your mind."

"May I ask you a personal question?"

"Go right ahead."

"How have you and Uncle Raymond managed to stay married so long?"

"Three things—compromise, compromise, and compromise. You can't have a good relationship with two people running in opposite directions. We've had lots of issues over the years. We were separated early on in our relationship."

I spring up. "When?"

"You were small. We had a little tiff because I didn't want to join Ray when he was stationed in Virginia. He went to Norfolk; I stayed in Sparta. Then there was the time I got a wild hair up my butt and decided I didn't need him or any other man to make it. I was a bonafide nurse practitioner and I didn't need *his* money."

"No way!"

"Yes, ma'am."

"Money problems, family issues, petty disagreements, you name it, we've been through it. I vowed to stick with him, though. I meant it when I said for better or worse. People don't take their vows as seriously today. They run at the first sign of trouble and wonder why marriage after marriage keeps failing." I hug my knees at her revelations. "I never said anything to you, Toni, but I'm glad Lamonte dipped out. I understand it takes a special man to accept a woman with mental illness in the family, but he was too big of a coward to give you a chance. You deserve better."

Willa sticks her head in the door. "You all right, Gumdrop?"

"Yeah, Willadean."

"Willa."

"If I'm Gumdrop, you're Willadean."

"Sounds like old times," Aunt Mavis says. She pats a spot on the bed and beckons Willa to join us. Willa sips her mug of coffee.

I can't believe Aunt Mavis and Willa. "You two are still coffee drinkers. I never got into all that caffeine, creamer, and sugar."

Willa looks at my bottle of brandy in the corner. "Mmm-hmmm," she says, and takes a longer sip. She turns to Aunt Mavis. "So what's today's street team plan?"

"We sell until we're done, then we take orders if necessary."

Remembering the curtains she'd sewn the past few days, I ask, "Did Uncle Raymond set up the pantry?"

"Last night. We were downtown until one this morning getting everything together. I finally finished the curtains and managed to tack the rod on the wood."

The matching curtains, labels, and Whiplash's cheerleading outfit display cartoon caricatures of May, Ray, and Whiplash. The bold font reads *May and Ray's Preserves*. We pasted the jars with the decorative pink, brown, and black labels. The preserves are permanent fixtures at the festival.

After breakfast, we caravan to the festival with my aunt and uncle leading the way. Donald entertains us with tales from his job and McKenna is bent over in a texting frenzy. Between her laughing and harrumphs, I deduce she's still dating Uriah. She taps my shoulder and shows me a photo of him at the beach surrounded by other teens.

"He's cute."

"He's a'ight."

Donald gives her the protective daddy look in the rearview mirror, and she sinks lower in her seat.

We arrive at our booth as others are setting up around us. The smell of delectable food wafts around the courthouse square. A band does a soundcheck on a heavy, wooden stage set up in back of the courthouse. Vendors untwist power cords, check food temperatures, and unpack cases of CDs and DVDs. Our home church, St. John's A.M.E., loads huge cakes on their table, as well as assemble quilt raffle tickets. Near the stage, carnival workers give one last test run for the two most popular rides—the Dragon Wagon and the Kite Flyer.

Willa flings an apron in my direction. "Put this on."

She tosses everyone else an apron as well. Donald opens Ball jar boxes and we each fill the pantry with goods, unfold the plastic May and Ray logo bags, and get ready for a long day. Everyone around us speaks to each other, and I almost forget that today I was supposed to say *I do.*

I bend down to pick up the cash box and credit card machine. When I stand again, a cheerful woman stares at me. "How may I help you, ma'am?"

"What time do you all start selling? May and Ray's is the first thing I buy every year."

"We officially start at ten, but if you tell me what you want, I can set it aside for you."

She looks around. "Where is ole' Whiplash? That dog gets a rise out of me every year. With her little freaky self." She laughs at her own joke. "I want the pepper jelly, some cucumbers, and a bottle of muscadine wine."

She opens her purse. Willa whispers in my ear, "Girl, that's not a purse, that's a pocketbook. An old, back-in-the-day one, like Mama and her friends carried."

I give her leg a soft kick and turn back to our customer. "You don't have to pay right now. I'll tuck it away for you." I get a box from beneath the table and place her requests inside.

"I pay for what I want upfront. You might slick me and act like I didn't come by here. Supply and demand, honey." She holds a twenty and her age-spotted hands tremble. The money lingers in her hands as she looks from me to Willa. "Y'all are Paul and Greta's girls, right?"

"Yes, ma'am," we respond in unison.

I gear up for another showdown like the one I had in IGA. She swings her big bag on the opposite shoulder like Shirley. She pulls on her red muumuu and twists her string of pearls, as if seeing us for the first time.

"Well, I declare! I hadn't seen y'all since you were practically babies. I lived down on Linton Road next to your Grandma Rose and Granddaddy Horace years ago."

"We were always forbidden to see them," Willa says.

"I know all about it. Wasn't right how Rose was left to fend for herself. Horace did the best he could, but Rose was sick and sick with it."

Donald steps in. "Hello, ma'am. I'm Willa's husband, Donald."

"I haven't even said my name yet. I'm Creasy Taylor. Been knowing the McCallisters for years."

"I'm sure my wife and sister-in-law would love to chat with you. Sounds like you know a lot about the family."

"I'm a walking encyclopedia of Hancock County, the Sparta Griot. Ain't a family I don't know about 'round here."

"You know our cousin, Edwina, correct?"

"Girl, yes. 'Wina is Grady's daughter. I knew Norlyza and Carrie Bell before they left here, too."

"We aren't supposed to sell until ten, but Ms. Creasy, we'll give you your items now if you promise to come back and chat later," I say.

"You don't have to bribe me. It'll be my pleasure. Y'all lived cooped up with too much secrecy anyway." I take her money and give her the small box. "You got any newspaper to wrap my wine? I don't want my nosy church members peeking in my box. Ain't none'a their business what I buy."

"Ms. Creasy, you are a mess!"

"I'm telling the truth, though. There's a difference between saints and ain'ts. Jesus was the life of the party, always drinking wine and having fun. But you can't tell the saints that."

"Give me your bottle," I say. I mummy-wrap her wine with the *Union Recorder* and stuff it in the box. She meanders to other booths, her muumuu blowing in the breeze.

A woman across from us stands at the DJ Cheese DVD booth. She smiles and I recognize her immediately. I get her attention, and she approaches our booth with tiny steps. Her embarrassment is evident as she bites her bottom lip and fiddles with our logoed tablecloth.

I shatter the silence with a hug. "Cousin Lorene, it's good to see you!"

Willa looks up from counting the till and follows suit. We group hug with a flimsy show of emotion from Lorene. The tighter we hug, the more she relaxes.

She steps back and gives us a head-to-toe scan. "You have grown into beautiful young ladies."

"You still look like a teenager, Cousin Lorene."

She blushes at the statement and flashes her signature, pearly smile. As a physical education teacher, she hounded us about hygiene, flossing, and exercise. When she was still married to Clay, we spent the night at their house, and when I refused to floss, she made me glide the string through my teeth, then sniff it. "If you can smell that, imagine what others smell," she said.

I purchase floss in bulk at Costco because of Lorene. Willa introduces her to Donald and McKenna. After which, we step aside and chat.

Lorene removes her wide straw hat, revealing a shaved head. Her skin is darker, but glowing.

"Chemo. I'm better now. There is a great support group of women here in Sparta who look out for me."

"We're sorry, Cousin Lorene. Aunt Mavis didn't tell us."

"Not a lot of people knew when I was first diagnosed, and not too many people know now unless I'm not wearing a hat or a scarf on my head. Folks mean well, but I don't like everybody praying over me, and I sure don't like a lot of negativity."

I make eye contact since she's embarrassed. "I'm glad you're better."

She delays her words like a child in time-out counting to ten and asks, "How is Clayton?"

"I went to see him last week. He's packing up the house and moving to Florida."

"Is he still with…" Her voice trails off, still unable to say Russell's name.

"Yes, ma'am. They're still together."

She sighs and fans her face with the hat. I check her ring finger to see if she's remarried, but it is void of a band of gold.

"Cousin Lorene, did you ever remarry?" Willa asks.

"Clayton Kenneth Myles was the only man I loved. I went back and forth about it, believing it was a phase. I don't care what people say about me behind my back; when we were good, we were good together. Him leaving me for a man knocked the wind out of me, you know."

The tables have shifted. When we were growing up, adults never made confessions to children. We're not children anymore, so Cousin Lorene sprinkles wisdom our way.

"I heard about what happened at the Blue Willow Inn," she says. I bite my bottom lip now. "Yep. Left at the altar."

"He wasn't for you. A man who really loves you loves all of you. Remember that, ya hear?"

"Yes, ma'am."

"Give me some of Mavis's goodies. Two pepper jellies, pickled peaches, and cucumbers, please." We bag her items and take her money. "You all down at the home-house?"

"Yes. I'm picking Mama up from the hospital Monday."

"Is it okay if I stop by to say hello sometimes?"

"Our doors are always open."

"Honey, open-door policies went away with cassette tapes. I don't drop in on people like I used to. Might get my feelings hurt."

That's exactly what led to her divorce. This is the story I gathered eavesdropping when Aunt Mavis's friends sat on her porch one night: Clayton packed for the Georgia Association of Educators conference and assured Lorene he'd be back in time for their anniversary dinner. His mistake was telling her he'd stop by their Atlanta house to check on the property. They spent their summer breaks in Atlanta in the home her parents had given them as a wedding gift. Her parents should have given her the middle name, Surprise. She had a reputation for popping in unannounced with gifts and trinkets for people.

In she waltzed, carrying a bouquet of daisies, a picnic basket, and Clay's favorite Manischewitz Blackberry wine. She stood in the living room, head cocked to the side, while Clay sat in Russ's lap eating cheese and purple globe grapes. As Russ bounced Clay on his knee and serenaded him with Marvin Gaye's "Soon I'll Be Loving You Again," she dropped the bottle, opened the picnic basket, and tossed food at them. Sandwiches, sweets, and fruit littered the living room floor. Near-sighted and living with astigmatism, she dropped her glasses, but felt around on the floor for the daisies.

She followed the sound of Clayton's voice saying, "Lorene, it's not what you think." She cold-cocked Russ in his mouth, chipping his tooth.

She backed away from them screaming and crying, "What don't I understand, *Clayton*? That you like sausages instead of pancakes!" She found her glasses and left the two of them there, filing for divorce the following week.

I assure her, "Your doors were always open for us, so the rules haven't changed. You're still Cousin Lorene, and you're still welcome to stop in anytime."

"Glad to know it," she says. She moves along, heartbreak covering her face.

The morning is starting off with a bang. It only gets better when I see Ethan's handsome face devouring a bag of blue cotton candy.

Chapter 20

I wave to Ethan and he looks past me. A handsome, lighter, teenage version of Ethan reaches across him as a woman in the food stand hands him a pretzel dog. The teen wears a red Baldwin High School T-shirt with an Indian sporting a Mohawk. The teen steps back as I try to get Ethan's attention again. This time, he gives me a slack wave and turns his attention back to the food stand. I look around for his wife. I don't want to be disrespectful, but it's good seeing him again and I want to tell him so.

"Willa, will you watch the booth? I'm going to speak to someone."

"Who do you know in this town after all these years?"

I point to Ethan. Willa's expression is a question mark. "He's Mama's social worker. He was at the meeting two weeks ago."

"Go ahead." She hands me a ten-dollar bill. "Bring me a pretzel dog and some popcorn, please."

The streets are swollen with people. I snake my way through the maze and tap Ethan's shoulder. "How are you? It's good to see you." He pauses a few seconds. "I'm Toni. Greta's daughter. We met a few weeks ago."

"I—"

"It's the hair, isn't it? I had it out and flowing the first time. These braids are necessary for this weather. October in Georgia is still warm."

"Dad, I'm going to mingle. Cuties abound." Ethan and his son do a fist pound.

"Son, you've got two hours to roam free. Meet me on the court-house steps in two hours."

Ethan turns his attention to me again. His left finger is void of its ring. It's too soon to be trouble in paradise. "Do we know each other?"

"*Hello.* We met at GMH."

"Oh, you mean—"

"Harassing the ladies, bro?" a voice asks.

Humiliation fills me. They stand next to each other and my mouth is agape.

"I'm Evan. I think you thought I was my twin brother, Ethan. He's the educated big head in the family. I'm just a handyman."

Ethan greets me again with his wife and children in tow. "Toni, when you mentioned the festival, I had no idea you'd be front and center." He points to my apron and quickly acknowledges his family. "This is my wife, Madeline, and my son, Calvin, and my daughter, Cheris." They shake my hand. Calvin and Cheris sport braces and preteen acne. Madeline smiles as well and looks lovingly at Ethan. "Toni is a relative of one of my clients."

"I'm sorry for the mix-up," I tell Evan. "You must have thought I was a bumbling idiot."

"Happens a lot. Don't be embarrassed."

"We're just starting with our booth search," says Ethan. "We'll leave you two alone."

They walk away and I realize I'm in the presence of a man again. Ethan and Evan are identical twins, and the electricity I felt at GMH returns. My face warms as I take in Evan's rugged good looks. I reach in my pocket, feel the ten-dollar bill, and look at our booth. Willa glares at me and pretends to shovel food in her mouth from an invisible plate.

"I have to get food for my sister."

"Let me help you."

We stand in line and I smell Evan's cologne. It's not Ethan's and Lamonte's, but I like it on him.

"Are you from here?"

"I was. I moved away years ago to Atlanta. And you?"

"We moved to Milledgeville from Athens our eighth-grade year. Our parents split and Mom moved closer to her relatives."

Children of divorce. Commonality number one. "I'm sorry, Evan."

"Don't be. They're much better friends than husband and wife."

"My parents are divorced and haven't spoken in years."

"Hopefully, you won't be like me when you get married. I'm divorced like my parents. My ex and I sound like your parents, no love lost between us."

"At least someone married you. Imagine getting dropped at your engagement party." I say this louder than I meant and the sarcasm-laced comment isn't lost on Evan. I try to rein the bitterness back in. "That didn't come out right."

"Still tender, huh?"

"Today would have been my wedding day." *TMI, Toni. TMI.*

We move a few spaces up in the line. "You'll thank him for it later."

"Everyone says the same thing. I'm not convinced yet."

"Takes time to get over a relationship. Enjoy being single."

Finally, we get to the front of the line. I order Willa's food and Evan pays for it before I can protest.

"Would you like something to eat?"

"I'm not really hungry, but thank you."

"How about dinner another time?"

The reason Lamonte left me comes to mind again. What man wants to date someone with crazy all up in their genes? Not Lamonte, and probably not Evan. Dating is good until you uncover the ins and outs of your life with someone. That's when men flee.

"I am tender. I'm not ready to date yet."

He feigns disappointment and covers his heart. "I. Can't. Make. It."

His antics generate laughter from us and the woman taking our order.

"You got a real comedian there, hun."

"He's not mine."

"Yet," Evan tells her.

I ignore his comment as we head back to the booth. We continue small talk as I give Willa her food.

"Toni tells me you're our mother's social worker. It's nice to meet you."

"Strike the earlier comment. This is his twin, Evan."

"Nice to meet you, Evan. You do have a last name, don't you?"

"Sutton."

He exchanges pleasantries with everyone and Aunt Mavis is just as shocked to learn Ethan has a twin.

"I feel like I've worried you enough. Let me find my son. He thinks he's the Don Juan of Central Georgia. I have to watch him like a hawk."

Willa nudges me to mingle with Evan. She gives me a slight push, but I push back. The butterflies in my stomach make me uncomfortable, and it's too soon to entertain the thought of being with someone else. I sense something in his countenance as well. He hasn't made a move to find his son yet.

"Would you walk me to my truck?"

Aunt Mavis speaks for me. "She'll go with you."

I'm outnumbered. I stroll around the courthouse square with Evan until we reach his F-150, parked near a car wash.

"Was I too forward earlier? If I was, I apologize."

"You were serious about dinner?"

"Yes."

"People small talk and speak in jest so much, I don't know when they're sincere."

"I am." He slips me a business card. The *S* in Sutton dangles from a hammer. Beneath his last name are his business and cell numbers. I read aloud, "Evan Sutton. Carpenter, Remodeler."

Commonality number 2. He's a building man.

"Evan, you don't know me from Adam's housecat. What makes you so sure you want to go out with me?"

"I dated Rhoda, my ex-wife, for fifteen years. We only stayed married three. I go for what I want now. There's something special about you and I want to get to know you better."

"I've got more baggage than Hermès. I'm not the one for you."

"Think about it, okay?"

I retie my apron straps. "I have to get back to the booth. It was nice meeting you." I head back to my selling duties at the booth.

"Call me when you have some time," he says to my back.

I'll call, all right. When I'm over this heartache and when my mother is schizophrenia-free.

Chapter 21

I sign the discharge papers and pack Mama's suitcase in the trunk, then go back in the building and wait for her to come down. My nerves are on edge, so I go outside, sit in the car, and wait. She finally emerges from the building carrying her teaching bag Daddy bought. Her gait is slower than usual, and for a split-second, I want to march her back to her room, drive to Atlanta, and pick up where I left off, damaged reputation and all.

Nurse Whipple escorts Mama to the car.

Mama's flat countenance scares me. "Is everything okay, Nurse Whipple?"

She points to an upstairs window, and a young woman presses her face against the glass. *Annalease.*

"She had dose of Depakote this morning. It's an extended release drug, so she'll be sleepy later. I've given you a list of her medications, dosages, and times she should take them. If she becomes noncompliant, call us immediately. As her guardian, and with her documented history, you can have her involuntarily hospitalized. Dr. Wells can sign the ten-thirteen if necessary."

"Ten-thirteen?"

"It's a form allowing Greta to be involuntarily transported to a treatment facility. That is, if she becomes a threat to herself or someone else."

"I doubt we'll need anything like that. She'll be okay."

I guide Mama to the passenger door and open it. Her gaze is fixed on Annalease. I back out of the parking lot and head home.

"What are we doing today?" she asks.

"We're going home and you're resting."

"What home?"

"The home-house. I was able to get it back for us. How does that sound?"

Her mouth twitches and she smirks. "You outwitted Mavis, didn't you?"

"Sure did."

"It's not falling in, is it?"

"No ma'am. It's been painted and restored to its old glory."

She will never hear Daddy's scheme from my lips. Nor will she see the booby traps I've planted to keep her in line. Mavis, Edwina, and her mental health professionals tell me I'm in for a bumpy ride. If she had been given more love and less meds, she might not be in this predicament. I placed a camera or two in the house to monitor her, and I'll spend time with her as she transitions to the mother I knew before the Hatcher Square Mall incident.

"Stop a minute over the hill."

We are across from the chapel again, in front of the pecan tree. The tree gives her life and she perks up. She pulls several reusable Piggly Wiggly bags from her briefcase. Lamonte and I never went to the grocery store without them and I'm impressed she ditched plastic.

"I'm going to pick us a few bags of nuts for pies and bars."

"Good. I missed your desserts. You know my baking and cooking skills are a little off."

"I'll fix that this time around."

We head toward the scattered nuts and pick several bags. She hums a familiar tune, rests, then continues.

"Go back to the car and let me finish this. You seem tired."

"I'm a little sleepy. I can finish picking my nuts, though."

"Mama, rest in the car. You'll have plenty of time to do all the things you like doing."

"How long am I staying with you?"

"Three months. This is a trial stay. If all goes well, we'll work on a permanent stay."

She beams. "I don't ever want to come back to this place."

"If I have my way, you won't."

With hesitance, she trudges back to the car. I watch her sit down, recline the seat, and close her eyes. She is not in a catatonic state, and I want to ensure she's not confined to the house. Aunt Mavis sat down with me a week ago and wrote out an activity plan for us to follow. I don't want a bunch of outsiders intruding on us, but I did agree to let cousin Edwina stop by to check on us since she is aware of the situation. Mama's been gone a long time; the Shirleys of Sparta can stay away from us with their gossiping and rumors.

The moment I open the door and place the pecan bags on the backseat floor, her eyes spring open. She is in a chatty mood. She opens her bag and hands me a piece of paper. I look at the document and recognize its purpose.

"This is my Voc Rehab completion certificate. I did their job training program over a year ago when I was taking my medication. I hope I can find a job. At least do something until I can get back in the classroom again."

I can't burst her bubble so soon. She'll never set foot in a classroom again. Not to teach, anyway. Aunt Mavis told me to avoid the topic if possible.

"I planned to surprise you with the job news later tonight. We have a job lined up for you starting two weeks from today."

"In the classroom?"

"Not exactly. It is at a local factory—"

"Factory? I don't want to do factory work."

"You didn't let me finish."

She sighs and scratches her arms. She's so irritated she diverts her attention to the window. She lets it up and down until I lock it.

"A local philanthropist rehabbed the Payback Factory. They contracted with a printing company and farmed out the work to Ray of Hope."

"Ray of Hope?"

"Your new job. You'll have a four-hour shift, Monday through Friday. I'll drop you off at eight in the morning and pick you up at noon. They make posters, calendars, bookmarks. Assembly tasks."

"Sounds like baby work to me."

"It's not baby work. You'll get adjusted to the routine of working again."

"Then I can teach?"

I cross my fingers so tight they're damn near a Celtic knot. "We'll see."

"I miss being in the classroom. The smell of chalk, the feel of the chalkboard, the kids' inquisitive eyes and questions. Do you know how it feels to explain a concept and see eyes light up when a person gets it?"

"I do."

"I don't want this work assignment to stretch out too long. I'll go to the Board of Education if I have to, and discuss getting a teaching assignment. Will you help me decorate my room?"

"I'm not good at decorating classrooms. Houses, yes."

"It's the same principle. You cut out decorative borders, block letters, all those things that make the classroom appealing to the students."

"Decorations have changed. A lot of those items are pre-cut now."

"You saying I'm ancient?" she snips.

"I didn't mean anything negative." This is going to be a long journey. Her students were like her children. Her brows are furled, a clear indication I've offended her. "Give Me Five."

Her facial muscles relax. "Hands to self, mouths quiet, eyes looking, ears listening, and hearts caring."

"You remembered!"

"I'm shocked *you* remembered."

"You posted Give Me Five in our bedroom and made us learn those principles when we were small. You said we weren't going to embarrass you and Daddy."

She's solemn again. She reaches for the radio, but her fingers fall near the power button. She sits back and hums a tune. Panic fills me. The rise and fall of her voice as she hums takes me back to Sunday morning breakfasts. The tune is "God Put a Rainbow in the Sky" by Mahalia Jackson, and she played it over and over again after Daddy left. I lured her away from the overcooked eggs and burned bacon by telling her I wanted candy. I'd give her the laced M&Ms, two-step her to the La-Z-Boy, and run back to the kitchen in time to toss the burned food in the trash.

We near downtown Sparta and I swing a left at the courthouse square. She needs to see her new place of employment, get a feel of the town again. A few people wave and some blow their horns. Ray of Hope is less than a mile, but she's fallen asleep. I continue on to the house.

We are secluded in the country, with a few neighbors here and there. The open farm and cattle land from my childhood is overgrown with trees. Willa and I looked out across the field in our yard to cows grazing most mornings. In the weeks I've been at our home-house, I cleaned and spray-painted the vintage glider and chairs, replaced the cushions, and bought a new table. We'll spend our evenings on the front porch listening to cicadas and fanning fireflies when the summer arrives next year. It won't be like the old days, but we can spend our time learning each other again.

Someone has been in our yard. There are bags and boxes on the front porch. I coast into the yard and park while she naps. If someone has stolen something, or is pranking us, I'll call the sheriff and we'll move to Aunt Mavis's.

I tiptoe up the steps, half expecting someone to jump out from the opposite side of the wraparound porch. I'm awash in relief as I search the contents of each bag. Fresh collards, turnips, onions, tomatoes, and beets fill the bags. A potted mother-in-law's tongue— her favorite plant—sits off to itself and is tied with a bright yellow bow. A box contains glass jars. I look for May and Ray's Preserves labels, but these are Mason jars, not Aunt Mavis's Ball jars. The top of each jar is labeled with a recipe and instructions. I turn the jars to find pancake, bread, seasoning, tea, and cocoa mixes. Gift tags with shaved red ribbons are wrapped around each jar. They read, *To: Greta, From: All of Us.* I rip open the envelope inside the box and read the handwritten message aloud.

We heard Greta was coming home and we wanted to give you a little something to help out. You both are in our thoughts and prayers. We love you.

Your friends and family in Hancock County
Chivalry may be dead, but Southern hospitality isn't.

Chapter 22

Greta

I enjoy the concert. Jesus directs the choir as 'Halia plays the piano and sings. It is a floating concert, like when Jesus walked on the water. Everybody is on the water, but nobody sinks. She jumps from song to song in a royal-blue robe. Her shoulders and back whirligig and dip the harder she hits the keys. She sings "Move on Up a Little Higher," then "How I Got Over" and after that, "In the Upper Room." The pews show no trace of water, but the spirit is high. A big man in a green toga and a crown of fig leaves clashes silver tambourines so heavy they sound like thunderclaps. I am on the front pew, rocking to the music, feeling the spirit. My mother, dressed in her favorite peach suit and pillbox hat, sneaks peeks at me and fans her face, creating a flowing effect with the lace in front of the hat.

The music stops, and Jesus motions for me to join him in the choir stand. As I rise, someone taps me on my shoulder. I turn around and it's Clark. He winks, slicks his hair, and wipes invisible lint from his suit.

I float on the water toward Jesus. 'Halia does a quiet-down move with her arms, and the music stops. Toga man places the crown of fig leaves on my head and floats back to his spot near the drummers. I wait for Him to speak, but He is silent.

"Jesus, where have you been?" Silence. "I feel like you've been gone forever. No one visits me anymore."

'Halia floats from the piano to a spot next to me. "You been doing all right?"

I nod. "I miss you coming to visit me."

The blue tint of her robe sparkles like the water around us. She turns away.

An eternity passes before Jesus takes my hand, leads me to the edge of the world. It's like a huge cliff. I look down and see flowers, trees, houses, people, and cars. They are small ants, moving at a rapid pace.

"Do you love me?" He asks.

"Of course, Jesus."

"Do you love me?"

"Yes."

"Will you keep my commandments?"

"I will."

He guides us away from the cliff and we are seated near 'Halia again. I look into his fiery eyes.

"If you love me, us, and want to see us again, don't take your medication. It makes it difficult for us to visit with you."

I touch His wooly hair and concede, "I understand, Jesus. I understand."

Chapter 23

Mama went to sleep with Mahalia Jackson on her tongue, and she awakens with Jesus on her mind.

She jerks and claws the dashboard. "Jesus, Jesus, Jesus!" Her chest heaves as she gasps for air. "Where are we?"

"Home."

She touches her feet. "They're dry. After all that water, how can they be dry?" She taps the CD player. "What happened to the music?"

"I turned it off so you could sleep."

She eases back into the seat and gawks at the house and yard. "Nothing's changed."

She hops out of her seat and roams the yard. She runs her hands over the plants, the garden fountain, and the yard light pole. May and Ray avoided drive-bys to the home-house when they picked her up. Said the memories would overwhelm her. The memories must be fond because her face brightens as she trots from one end of the yard to the other. She folds her hands behind her back and slows her pace. She disappears to the backyard. I'm sure she's in search of the old well and the fish cleaning table.

Aunt Mavis rings my cell. "How are things so far?"

"She's in disbelief. She's really shocked the house is still standing."

"You didn't tell her anything, did you?"

"My lips are sealed."

"If she takes her meds and improves, we can discuss transferring ownership back to her."

"Aunt Mavis, I'm taking this one day at a time. Make that one hour at a time."

"I like that attitude."

"Are you and Uncle Ray driving out tonight?"

"No. You two need to bond." Whiplash barks and yips. "Go drink your water, Whiplash." After a moment of silence, she returns. "Has Willa changed her mind?"

"Not yet. I'm working on her, though. Maybe she'll come to the fish fry we're having."

"Call us if you need anything."

"Thanks for helping me bring her home."

I end the call as Mama walks around the side of the house. I join her and we walk arm-in-arm toward the steps. She drags the potted mother-in-law tongue next the food.

"Whose food is this?" She digs through the bags and the box. "These collards are fresh." She thumps the leaves. "And hardy, too. First frost fell on them well."

"They're yours."

"Who left them?"

"Family and friends. Let's take them inside." We enter the house and she stops in the foyer.

Her eyes find Mr. Juggles. "Juggles is still giving out fortunes, huh?"

"He is."

She lifts his head and fishes around for a fortune. She plucks one out and reads it aloud. *"Courtesy is contagious."* She puts the fortune back and walks into the living room.

"Let me put these bags in the kitchen. I'll be right back."

After dropping the bags off, I walk back to the living room. Her countenance has changed again and she flashes a look of anger.

"Who took the plastic off my furniture?"

"Mama, no one ever sat in here." I remember my role as co-conspirator with Aunt Mavis and add, "I had it steam-cleaned. Go ahead, touch it. Sniff it, even."

She sniffs and relaxes. She sits down on the sofa and kicks her feet up on the coffee table, a move forbidden when we lived here.

"Hand me those photo albums in the bottom drawer."

Unsure if Aunt Mavis moved them, I proceed with caution and crossed fingers. I slide the door open and breathe. They're still here. I pass them to her.

"I'm going down memory lane a while. You sitting with me?"

Aunt Mavis rings my cell again.

"Let me get this. Be right back." I take her call on the porch. I nestle in the glider and cross my legs. "Did you forget something?"

"Some flowers arrived for you. Do you want me to drop them off?"

I bolt upright. Maybe Lamonte's apologizing. He owes me that much. "Is there a card with them?"

"Yes. Do you want me to read it?"

She may as well hear what he has to say, too. "Sure."

She pauses a moment, then reads, *"Toni. I'm back from Italy and saw the article. Call me when you're ready to talk. I'm always here. Friends forever. Jordan.* She sent a large colorful bouquet. These would make a beautiful display on Greta's dining room table. I'll keep them fresh until you pick them up."

"Thanks, Aunt Mavis."

"What's wrong?"

"I thought they were from Lamonte."

"Not to sound harsh, but he's moved on. So should you. You have a lot on your plate, but we can always watch Greta while you carve out some me time."

Mama sticks her head out of the screen door. "I'm going to clean the greens so I can cook."

"Aunt Mavis, let me call you back."

She practically staggers as I fall in step behind her. Nurse Whipple had explained the extended dosage would kick in after a few hours. The effects are evident. I guide her toward the guest bedroom and sit her on the edge of the bed.

"You are a good daughter. I'm sorry about the things I said about you in the paper."

Her speech isn't slurred, but it is slower, more pronounced.

"You need to sleep. I wanted to talk to you about the fish fry, though."

"We're still having it, right?" She grabs a pillow and cradles it, groggier now. "What's it for again?"

"Celebrating your homecoming and your new job at Ray of Hope."

"That's right."

"A few people are coming to say hi. They won't tucker you out. They'll just say hi, eat a little bit, and go home."

She waves her hands and sings, "…Will be always howdy howdy, and never goodbye. 'Halia taught me to sing it just like she does."

She's down for the count. I take her shoes off and scoot her body closer to the head of the bed. I fluff the pillows.

"Who's coming?" she asks.

"Cousin Edwina and Walter, Lorene, some of the ladies from St. John's."

She yawns. "Who else?"

"May, Ray, and Whiplash."

"I love Whiplash. She is May and Ray's granddoggy. Who else?"

I clear my throat. "Willa, her husband, Don, and your grand-daughter, McKenna."

She turns her back to me. Through a Depakote-induced haze, she says, "Hide my food when Willa comes. Wrap it up in aluminum foil and put it in the microwave."

I rub her back. "I will, Mama."

Chapter 24

Mama swigs her second goblet of muscadine wine as she dresses catfish filet, tilapia, and perch. Aunt Mavis offered to help us prepare the food, but Mama insisted on cooking since the fish fry is in her honor. The November weather warrants an inside fish fry. Truth is, she still balks at the idea of someone else's hands near her food. She leans over the sink rinsing red potatoes for her loaded potato salad as I squirt Woeber's honey mustard in the beef baked beans.

"Don't forget to crumble up the bacon in the beans," she says.

She is in her element. This is the mother I craved as a child, the mother in whose lap I'd curl and inhale her Chanel No. 5. She dons a sassy apron, the one she's worn the past two weeks, and fires off cooking commands.

"Mama, check the pound cake."

"You do it. Got my hands full. All you need to do is turn the light on and peek inside. Constantly opening the oven door will flatten that poor baby for sure."

"Yes, ma'am."

"Oh, put the decanters out. I'll mix passion punch in one and half and half in the other."

"I missed your passion punch."

"Thank to Whipple, I do it with a strawberry lemonade mix now instead of powdered Kool-Aid. Gives it a better flavor."

She tears a huge sheet of aluminum foil from an industrial-sized box and covers two baking sheets. "Pass the lemons." I give her lemons I'd emptied from bags earlier. "Did you squeeze them?"

"Forgot."

"The secret to good fried fish is the lemon juice. You don't need seasoning on the fish; that's why you let the juice marinate in the fish for an hour and season the cornmeal. Cut those lemons in half and squeeze the juice." She wipes her hand on her apron and demonstrates. She swipes a lemon from the bowl and glides it across the counter with her hand, running it back and forth until it softens. "See. It's soft now. Squeeze-ready."

"Please tell me who gave you the apron." The smart-alecky quips have me in stitches.

"May gave it to me years ago. You like it?"

"Sounds like all the women in our family." I read some of the sayings aloud. "Get your hands off your hips. You don't know what tired is. Wear clean underwear in case you have to go the hospital."

We laugh at the last saying because Aunt Mavis shared ER stories of ripped undies and stretched bras. I take the stainless steel bowl of lemons and press them.

An incoming call from Willa interrupts my lemon rolling. "Taking a call. Be right back."

"Are you close?" I ask as I walk to the dining room with the bowl.

"Getting off on exit one thirty-eight. You need anything before we get to the sticks?"

"Oh Progressive One, two bags of ice would be nice."

"Anything else?"

"A better attitude."

"You know I'm nervous about this. I'm doing this for you."

"Don't do it for me. It has to be for you. You have to be the bigger person."

"I don't want to be the bigger person. Midget is my middle name."

"Wouldn't you want someone to take care of you if you were sick?"

"Yes."

"Mama is sick. We have to look at it that way."

"She never accused you of poisoning her, though."

"She didn't mean it. She was sick then and she's sick now."

"Has she taken her medicine today?"

"I made sure she did."

"How do you know?"

"I stood outside the bathroom door and waited until she finished."

"If she says one thing out of the way, I'm going back to Birmingham."

"Toni, are you done with the lemons?" Mama calls from the kitchen.

"We're dressing the fish. I'll see you when you get here. I love you, Willa."

"Love you too, Toni."

My hands are red from squeezing as I take the bowl back to the kitchen. The cake cools on a wire rack. I reach for a knife, slice the lemons, and squeeze them over the fish. Mama grabs a brown paper bag from the pantry and scatters meal and seasonings inside. She drops the fish in a bag and puts the dredged pieces side by side on the baking sheets.

"Spread some Saran over the fish and put it in the fridge. I made us some lemonade so we can sit on the porch while the fish marinates."

"It's chilly out there. Let's sit in the den."

She takes a tray of lemonade and finger sandwiches to the den. We sit on the sofa and chat about different subjects. Curiosity drives her conversation.

"You never told me about the guy who dumped you."

I try not to take her comment personally. Aunt Mavis told me she would say or do things that weren't polite and to go with it.

"His name is Lamonte. He's an architect and lives in Conyers."

"Hmm, sounds like a good job." She sips her lemonade. "Does he have his own house?"

"Yes, ma'am."

"But you had your own place too, correct?"

"I do." She makes me nervous as she draws small circles on her legs. A far-off gaze overtakes her and her neck snaps.

"He sounds like your father. See, the world tells women to find a man with all these material things. But what about staying power? What about a man who's willing to weather storms with you or be there for you when you're not yourself?" She points to a saying on the apron and repeats it. "Buy a man a pair of shoes and he'll walk out on you."

She wants an amen, but I continue listening.

"I'm not saying those things don't matter. Shoot, it's a sorry dog that won't wag his own tail. I'm saying you need more than *things* to make a marriage work."

Tears stream down her face and I take her lemonade. "Let me take your apron while you get a nap."

She jerks her shoulder when I touch her. "You all are always trying to put me to sleep or dope me up with medication. Let me enjoy myself for a change."

I glance at my watch. "Willa should be here in a few minutes. She called when they got off the exit."

She follows me to the front porch. She grabs a jacket from the hall tree and paces near the oak tree. I bite my bottom lip when I see Don navigating their SUV over the hill. I didn't tell Willa the party starts at four. I said one. This gives us time to talk and relieve tension before the crowd arrives. He parks in front of the oak; Mama runs back to the porch and stands next to me. Don opens Willa's and McKenna's doors. Their steps are slow as they head toward the porch. I make eye contact with Willa and telepathically communicate, *Bigger person, bigger person.*

Mama meets Willa halfway in the yard. Willa hugs her and they fall into a loving embrace.

"Look at you. All grown up now. Thirty-eight years old and you don't look a day over twenty-five. Turn around." Willa unbuttons her fleece coat and exposes her casual outfit. "Still got those baby-making hips." She turns to Don. "Bet that's why you married her, didn't you?"

They both blush. "I married her because I love her and she's a good woman. The beauty was an added bonus."

Willa punches his arm. "Mama, this is my husband, Don, and my daughter, McKenna."

Mama reaches out to McKenna. "Come hug your grandmother."

McKenna is a statue. Willa pokes McKenna's side and tilts her head toward Mama. She finally takes two steps and wraps her arms around her grandmother.

"You sure are a pretty little thing. Your mother looked the same when she was your age. I heard you're into sports."

McKenna shifts her stance and unthaws. "I'm in traveling soccer and I want to play volleyball. Mom and Dad want to me concentrate on academics, though."

"Whatever you do, give it all you've got," Mama says. She is quiet, reflective. She disappears from us briefly with an odd look. She comes back to us and says, "It's good being here with you all." She points to the front door. "Let's have some lemonade."

McKenna's phone is hidden today and her attention is focused on family. Mama directs everyone to the den and continues chatting. She pours cups of lemonade and offers everyone sandwiches.

"You all live in Birmingham, right?"

"Yes, ma'am. I've been in Alabama since—"

Something inside Mama clicks. She cups her lemonade, rocks back and forth, and tilts back on the sofa. "Go on and say what you were about to say, Willa."

"Since I moved away. Birmingham's been good to us."

Mama wrings her hands and jumps up. "I need to check on the food in the kitchen."

Stunned, we sit in silence. I give them an apologetic look. "I'll go in and see about her. Give me a second."

The low mumbling of Mama's voice seeps from the kitchen. She paces back and forth. Aware I'm near, she continues. "Told you she couldn't be trusted."

"What are you talking about?"

"The poison. She has it in her pockets. 'Halia told me."

"She doesn't have anything in her pockets."

"You don't see it because she can make it invisible. She has that arsenic and those D-Con pellets." I reach out to her. "Don't put your hands on me! The longer she sits in here, the better chance she'll have to kill me. Look at all this food. She can come in here and take us out like an assassin!" Her voice raises several octaves.

I back away from her and call Willa. The three of them come quickly from the den and stand in the kitchen doorway.

I walk toward Mama. "Do you really think she'd drive three hours with her family to poison you?"

"I sure do. She came back to finish what she started all those years ago." She moves toward Willa and the kitchen door, away from me, but I can't let her leave. I don't want her to harm herself or Willa.

I hold my hands up in surrender. "Come sit down and talk to

me about it. I'll get the poison from Willa and make sure I cover your food the whole time she's here."

"See how you're defending her? You'd pick *her* over *me*!" She points to Willa. Don kneads her shoulders, and the three of them assume their leaden stance.

"I'm not taking sides. We can sit down and talk about this." Aunt Mavis and Cousin Clayton's premonitions come full circle. I can't handle her break from reality.

"Yes, you are. You see she is trying to kill me and you don't care. I thought you were the good daughter, the one who had my back!"

She stalks to the refrigerator, bends down, and rises with a jar of pickles. She hurls the jar at me and I duck. It narrowly misses my ear and crashes on the cabinet. Glass and pickle juice surround me.

"Mama, you have to calm down!" In my brain, the words were softer, but my tongue expresses my true feelings. Raw fear bubbles inside me.

"I don't have to do a damn thing! You probably plotted with her to get me out of the hospital." She turns her back to us and breathes heavily at the sink. Her shoulders heave as she whispers unintelligible phrases and coughs.

How do you know she took her medicine? Willa's question pricks me as I head to the bathroom to check the Zyprexa bottle.

"McKenna, go outside." To Don and Willa, I say, "Call Aunt Mavis and dial nine-one-one."

Don remains in the doorway while Willa fumbles in her purse for her phone. There is no way she'd react this way if she'd taken her meds. I'd allowed her to go to the bathroom on the honor system to take her medication the past two weeks. I pop the cap off the bottle and count the pills. Sixteen remain, the accurate number per her dosage.

I go back to the kitchen, keeping my distance as she stands near the sink. "Empty your pockets."

She whips her head around. "What for?"

"If Willa has something in her pockets, then it's fair that I check yours to make sure you're not planning to do anything to her."

"No!"

I pretend to leave, then double back, slipping my hands into her apron pockets. Her pills are in hiding in Saran Wrap in a knot. I snatch them out and point them in her face.

"Yes, I took my meds, Toni!" I mock her earlier profession.

"Give me back my medicine!" She slams her fist on the counter, then spits in my face. I pivot toward the paper towels as spittle drips. Outraged, she topples me from behind, her fist pounds raining on my back and face. I kick as Don pulls her off me.

She stops wrestling against Don's strong arms. We wait for Aunt Mavis, an ambulance, someone, to arrive. My back is sore and my face aches.

Still restrained by Don, Mama sits in a chair where she whispers over and over, "Howdy howdy, and never goodbye."

Chapter 25

Ethan joins us in a small room at Oconee Regional Medical Center ER. Not only is Willa still here, but she rubs my back and applies an ice pack to my face. She morphs into the protective mechanism of our youth and fields questions from Ethan.

"Can you tell me what happened again, Willa?"

"We were in the den, Mama got antsy and went to the kitchen."

"Once inside?"

"I overheard Mama saying something about me poisoning her. Toni called me into the kitchen, and things got crazy. Next thing I knew, Mama was pounding Toni on the floor." Willa holds me tighter.

"Toni, do you feel like talking about it?"

I shift in my seat. "She was doing well. She prepared food like she did when we were younger. She sipped wine, dressed the fish—"

"Wine?"

"A little muscadine wine."

"Alcohol is dangerous. It's toxic with medication, and she shouldn't drink it given her mental state."

"I can't believe I was so stupid."

"You didn't know. That's why I need to know what led to the outburst."

"She went to the kitchen, and when I got there, she paced back and forth." I stare straight ahead, not wanting to make eye contact with Willa. "She said Willa had invisible poison in her pocket and planned to put it in our food. She was scared."

Ethan scribbled notes in a leather binder. "How did the clinical follow-up visit go?"

"Follow-up?"

"Yes. As part of the discharge agreement, you signed documents stating you'd take her to weekly visits at Vinings Mental Health Services." He rifles through papers in the binder and presents a signed copy of the document. "Here." He points to my signature.

My signature is there, fancy loops and lines. Did I really think I could gallop in on my daughter horse and rescue my mom from this disease? Lying—my friend, my lover, my confidante, my shield—won't work this time.

"Ethan, I asked her about the visit and she said she felt fine. She said as long as she took the medication, she didn't have to go to the clinic."

The creases in his forehead deepen as he glides his tongue over his teeth. He rubs his bald head and clicks the pen he's holding. "Toni." He speaks as if I'm eight. "She can't negotiate the moves. The weekly visits are to assure she's taking her medication. Think of the visits as wellness checks. Blood may be drawn to see what's in her system, and if she's not taking the meds, a weekly injection can be done to make sure she's stabilized."

Willa pulls me closer. "This thing with her requires a long learning curve. Maybe you should—"

"Maybe I should what? Dump her at GMH again?"

"No, I was going to say let Aunt Mavis help you out until January. You're not equipped to take care of her yet."

Stamp "F" on my forehead for failure. My fantasy, this reunion where my mother would be cured and able to carry on as if nothing ever happened, is a wash.

Ethan lulls me back. "The family has to determine your next steps."

"Next steps?"

"Toni, you need to decide if you'll fully immerse yourself in taking care of her or send her back to GMH."

"No. I promised her three months."

"Look at your face."

I hold the ice pack closer. "It's my fault she's here now."

"Don't blame yourself, Toni," Willa says.

"I shouldn't have let her go in the bathroom alone. I trusted her when she said she was taking the pills."

"Toni, she's been hiding pills under her tongue for years," Ethan says. "She knew you were unaware of her habits, so she slipped them in her pocket. Two weeks is a long time to be without meds. That's what triggered the episode."

"What am I supposed to do now?"

Ethan slides me a form. I read it, shake my head, and give it back to him. "I'm not giving Dr. Wells permission to sign this ten-thirteen."

"Toni, you're in no position to care for her right now. You need more education on the subject matter. We have a local NAMI chapter and another support group, Beacon Cottage. Both offer family support meetings. You can't do this alone. Beacon was formed by a consumer mother after her daughter died in the care of the state." He removes a cardholder from his jacket. "Beacon's address is on the front, and I will write your names on the back. It is a referral-only admittance group. They meet the last Thursday of every month. You and Willa should make arrangements to attend together."

Willa looks at the card. "I'll help out financially also."

I face my sister. "Willa…"

"Granted, I live out of town, but I'm willing to travel to help her. The one thing Norlyza and Carrie Bell always told me was how they let Uncle Grady down. In spite of the past, she's our mother. I didn't realize how vulnerable she is until today."

I squeeze her hand, pleased by her show of support. We both face Ethan.

I take the lead since I'm the reason we're here. "What are our options?"

"Meds and watching her like a hawk until she stabilizes."

Willa asks, "Has she been admitted?"

"She's still in an ER holding room."

Ethan stands and we follow him to her room. She sits up in a small bed talking with Dr. Wells. She is groggy, but answers his questions. Dr. Wells stands and shakes our hands.

Ethan speaks for us. "Dr. Wells, may they speak to her alone?"

He nods. "Come outside with me, Sutton."

We sit on her bed and take her by the hands. She averts her eyes, but speaks to us. "I'm sorry about today. I didn't mean to hurt you."

I speak for us. "We're here to help you. You can't get better if you won't let us help."

She tightens her grip on our hands and angles her body into an S-shape as she falls asleep.

Chapter 26

Christmas is three weeks away. After the fish fry that wasn't, we skipped Thanksgiving and are zooming into my mother's favorite holiday. Aunt Mavis and I made a pact—I can work my holiday designer mojo on the house for Christmas as long as I accompany them on the weekly Vinings checkups. Mama returns to the home-house tomorrow night. She's been staying with my aunt and uncle by choice. She said she wants enough medication in her system before she mingles with me again. Said she wants our bond to be stronger. I have roughly four hours to unpack the tree, decorate the house, and make it to the Beacon Cottage support group meeting.

I've gone back and forth about attending. The word *support* makes me feel weak, as if I can't navigate life without telling someone all my business. My shortcomings. It's not about me, though, and I recognize the only way to better the circumstances is to put my mother first.

The record player Daddy bought is still in the living room. So are all the albums my parents collected over the years. All slots of the wooden, vintage album holder are filled with golden oldies, huge albums with provocative covers that I listened to as a child. I take a few albums from the holder and blush. The Ohio Players' *Honey* album ticked Mama off. She said she wanted the woman on the cover to choke on the honey she held with the spoon. She didn't care for Millie Jackson sitting on the toilet either, but some-how, Millie's raunchy sister-girl sermons ministered to Mama when she thought Daddy was tipping out. I pull out our "day after Thanksgiving" anthem, "This Christmas" by Donny Hathaway. Before the Black Friday frenzy started in our household, Mama woke us up every year to this tune. I move on to decorations and splay boxes of lights on the living room floor. These haven't been unraveled in years, but I'm up for the challenge. I drop the needle on the .45 and bop my head to music. I close my eyes and sway to the rhythm so hard I wrap the lights around my body.

Donny's crooning and the instruments make me pretend I'm at a basement Christmas party. I'm so enthralled by the music I almost piss my pants from the knock on the living room window. The lights drop to my knees and feet as the woman stands pointing and laughing at me. I turn the music down, untangle myself, and unlock the front door.

"Is this how you handle life without me?" Jordan asks. She waltzes in with her bigger-than-life personality and moves past me with two large gift bags. She doesn't wait for an invitation to relax as she makes herself at home. "Where's the tree?" She tosses her coat over the sofa and sets the bags near the fireplace. Her face glows; she wears leggings, tan riding boots, and a cream cashmere sweater.

"Jordan. How—?"

"Text messages, flowers, cards. Did you really think I'd let the year end without laying eyes on you? Do you know what I plunked down for the maid-of-honor dress?" She bends to hug me, and I'm swept up in her latest perfume. "You're speechless. Serves you right for ignoring me."

When she sits on the sofa, the source of her glowing skin becomes apparent. She rubs her belly and gives me a *Now what?* look. Buddies since our sophomore year in high school, Jordan accepted me when other girls said Russ and Clay's homosexuality was contagious and they didn't want to catch it. She studied with me at the dining room table every night, and her parents took me on vacations, welcomed me into their home, and helped me transition from high school to college during the onset of Clay's emphysema. Her deep-set, brown, compassionate eyes make me feel like a bigger gyp. I kick the lights aside and plop next to her.

"Would you like something to eat or drink?"

"A face-to-face apology would be nice."

"I'm sorry, Jordan."

"Sorriest friend on the planet."

"I wanted to say something, but I didn't know—"

"Come on, Toni. A girl lives with two men, no mention of a mother, and vague references to her roots. I knew something was a little off."

"Why didn't you ever ask?"

"Too instrusive. If you wanted me to know, you would have said something. Now, I didn't expect to find out in the *AJC*, but after I read it, I understood why you were so secretive."

"Are you ashamed of me?"

"I'm a little sad you didn't trust me enough to open up, but we can move beyond this little misunderstanding if you give me the Sparta lowdown."

"What lowdown?"

"Sparta is the most compassionate place. Russ and Clay gave me Mavis's address a while back. After I drove here, I realized I'd left it on the counter. I stopped by a corner store, said Mavis's name, and the coolest man wearing a skull cap told me all your family history." She pulls out a slip of paper. "Gave me directions right up to your doorstep. Told me you were staying at the home-house." Instead of air quotes, she forms parentheses around home-house.

I flinch. "What was his name?"

"He said his name is Lucas Stewart. Of the…"

"Devereaux Stewarts," we say in unison.

"Atlanta has nothing on this town. People wave, speak, and make me feel like a superstar. I might have to raise your godchild here."

"Who's the stork?"

"Toni, I had a baker, not a stork. A sweet Italian man named Carlo. A little wine, some homemade spaghetti, sex on a moonlit balcony, and voilà." She rubs her little bun in the oven again and sidesteps the obvious question.

"What about Perry?"

"Perry shot blanks for years. What's a girl to do?"

"So you really meant it when you told me you wanted to raise a child alone?"

"All by my lonesome. I can afford it, and I have a bad daddy's girl syndrome. I doubt any man will ever live up to my father's image."

"A man isn't supposed to. You're supposed to form your own bond. By the way, how are your parents?"

"Disappointed they couldn't come to your wedding. Spill the tea. What happened?"

My comfort level with Jordan astounds me after all these years. "Instead of the altar, I got ditched at the engagement party."

"I told you that punk—"

I lift my hands in protest. "Don't. I'm moving past this one day at a time."

"A man with a head that big shouldn't be choosy. He was lucky you gave him the time of day."

"Spoken like a true friend."

"What did Clay say?"

"You know he wants me to be happy. He said if it doesn't fit, don't force it. He also wants me to concentrate on helping Mama get better."

She embraces me, something she rarely does. Her sarcasm and quick wit are what I've grown accustomed to over the years. "Don't give up without doing all you can for your mom. Russ told me about her struggles."

Her tender tone is foreign. I don't know this Jordan.

"I had this fairytale mindset about helping her. The saying 'Mental illness can be contained, not cured' is true. It's hard enough getting her to take meds. I haven't convinced her to see a psychologist yet."

"She's been on this journey a long time. She'll come around."

"I'm learning to cope, but it's hard. One minute she's lucent, the next minute she's talking to herself and accusing us of conspiracy theories."

"Give her time. I didn't come here to depress you. It's the holiday season." Jordan directs her gaze at the tree box and lights. "Need help decorating this naked room?"

"Like old times. Remember we decorated each other's houses every year? I miss my old place."

"Speaking of which, I stopped by your house when I got back from Italy, since you treated me like trash. Giovanna is taking excellent care of your place. You know how I feel about renting and tenants."

"Will you ever live down the Section Eight disaster?"

"No. I rented my house out in good faith and returned to stained carpets, holes in the wall, and candle wax on my countertops. I won't be renting to anyone again."

"I got lucky with Giovanna. I realized it when I did a few creep-ups on her."

"So, let's get this naked house looking Williamson Design-fabulous."

I fire up Christmas music as Jordan pushes off the sofa with her stomach. She unravels lights, helps assemble the tree, and tosses tinsel on the tree like confetti. We sing and dance as we string lights and holly along the mantel. I place Mama's favorite angel in the center of the fireplace. We stand back and admire our handiwork in the living room.

Jordan admires her handiwork. "This is fun. I have to go to Atlanta and do it all over again since I've procrastinated. I'm having trimester issues."

"I wish I could help you. I mean with decorating and the baby."

"Your place is with your mom now. I was afraid you wouldn't let me in when I showed up unannounced, but I wanted to tell you I love you, and nothing trumps my love for you as a friend."

"I want the mean Jordan back. This one makes me want to cry."

"Not so fast. I'm buttering you up for babysitting duties. Go with the sensitive me for now." Jordan grabs her coat.

"Why don't you spend the night? I'm here alone and I could use the company."

"I would if I hadn't promised Perry I'd meet him tonight. Can you believe he wants to discuss continuing our relationship in spite of me carrying another man's child?"

"You have been together a long time."

"We can be friends, but I doubt I'll ever be committed to anyone. Blame my father."

I help her put her coat on and walk her to the front door. She is the epitome of a true friend. Our friendship is the type that picks up where it left off, regardless of the time we've been apart.

"Are you ready for the meeting?" she asks as we head to her car.

"As ready as I'll ever be. I'm a little uncomfortable telling people my personal business, but I have to start somewhere. Outside of family, I've been secluded since the article ran."

"You can't stay locked away forever. There is a new design assignment out there with your name on it."

"Once I'm comfortable with the routine of taking care of my mother, I'll seek a freelance assignment or two."

"Let me know if you need me to help you out on my end. I'm a phone call away." She plants a kiss on my cheek and gets in her car. "Don't be a stranger."

I watch Jordan drive away, grateful to her for allowing me to be transparent about my mother. Quality beats quantity in friendship any day.

Chapter 27

Beacon Cottage is aptly named. The driveway in which I sit holds a lovely bungalow painted green and white. I'm a sucker for good design and curb appeal. Nothing gets me like good landscaping, and the owners of this home have made the grounds a winter wonderland. I find the referral card Ethan gave me and head toward the front porch. The meeting starts in twenty minutes, but he had suggested I come early. He said I don't have to talk if I'm uncomfortable, but it helps to express myself. I walk toward the porch and speak to a man smoking a cigarette in one of two Adirondack chairs. He stands to greet me as I near the door. He drags on the cigarette, blows smoke away from my face, and places it in the ashtray.

"How are you, tonight?" He extends a hand to shake mine. "I'm Jim Beacon. I haven't seen you here before."

"I'm Toni Williamson. I was referred by Ethan Sutton."

"Your name won't matter once you get inside. I'm glad you could join us tonight."

I release Jim's hands and notice his yellowing nails. His face is youthful, but gray hair covers his head. I'd venture to guess he's under forty, but his eyes are pools of sadness. The night carries a biting chill, but he is dressed only in corduroys and a striped flannel shirt. He shuffles his feet and finally says, "Go on inside. My wife will give you the skinny on the meeting."

I knock on the door and a happy-go-lucky woman answers it. She steps aside to let me in.

"Ethan sent you, didn't he?" she asks.

A quick sweep of the house tells me I'm among kindred spirits. She welcomes me in and I feel like I'm at Aunt Mavis's. She sets snacks on a buffet table in the living room and I fall in line with her. Chairs are placed in a semicircle and a podium sits off to the side.

"What do you need me to do?"

"I've done most of the finger foods. Let's get the snacks on the table. By the way, I'm Delores Beacon."

"Toni Williamson."

"Not sure if Jim told you, but you don't have to give your real name. I'll tell you about our format when we're done with the food."

I bring a pink box from Doddle's Cupcake Bakery from the kitchen. I rotate bowls of tortilla chips, salsa, cheese straws, and a tray of pinwheel sandwiches to the left of the buffet. The right side houses wrapped gifts and few Santa gift bags.

"Do you mind putting the cupcakes out?" I open the box so others can serve themselves. Delores chatters with me as we continue putting out the food. "I take it Ethan told you about our daughter?"

"He only said she died in the care of the state. He didn't go into details."

Delores's red holiday dress is festive, as are her candy cane earrings. Her hair is swept up in a bun with wisps of hair framing her face. She is the opposite of Jim tonight.

"Our ten-year-old daughter, Sherri, died when she was left too long without oxygen at a mental facility in North Georgia. Jim took it the hardest, as you can probably tell. Hair turned straight white before he turned thirty-five." She detects my sadness. "Don't be sad. I'm grateful for the short time we had with her. Our marriage has been fragile since she died two years ago, but I'm hoping Jim comes around and realizes she was on loan to us."

"I never thought of death that way."

"Everything is about mindset, Toni."

Delores removes the Santa Claus apron from her dress and we both walk to the kitchen.

"Our meetings are held once a month for family members dealing with grief or who are in the role of caregiver for a mentally ill family member. We have our usual mix of people, but someone new comes into the fold from time to time. There are two bowls of first names on the buffet. The pink bowl has female names and the blue bowl has male names. The name you select is who you'll be for the night. This provides anonymity, and to some degree, a measure of comfort. People can be uncomfortable shedding layers to strangers."

"Great idea."

"You can pull a name and wait for the others. Our December meeting is usually a thin crowd due to the holiday season."

I pull a name from the pink bowl. "Susan."

"I'll remember your new name for the night." Delores moves the podium in the center of the chairs. "Are you a caretaker or a bereaved family member?"

"Caretaker."

"I've been both, so I can appreciate you wanting to talk. We are here no longer than an hour, but I'm available if you'd like to talk alone."

"Sounds good. I don't even know if I'll be able to talk tonight."

"By the way, I always make a point to mention we aren't trying to steal NAMI's thunder. We are grassroots, also. All races and genders join us for meetings. Mental illness knows no race or socioeconomic boundaries. You can visit with us and them as well."

The doorbell rings and I realize I've become countrified the past six months. I no longer ring doorbells. I knock.

Delores opens the door and two women and a man file in. They are regulars. They hang up their coats, run to the buffet, and pick names from the bowls. They speak to me and take seats in the chairs. I hear an engine idling, and I look out the window. Jim backs out of the driveway.

We start the meeting with introductions.

"I'm Susan."

"Carlotta."

"Houston."

"Rita."

The members stand and I follow suit. Houston sidles next to me with a piece of paper. Delores takes her position as moderator at the podium. "Let us recite the motto."

Carlotta, Rita, and Delores know it by heart. Houston sticks by my side with the poem typed on a four-by-six glossy card. "If I can stop one heart from breaking/I shall not live in vain/If I can ease one life the aching/Or cool one pain/Or help one fainting robin/Unto his nest again/I shall not live in vain. Emily Dickinson."

We take our seats and Delores encourages us to speak. Carlotta's eyes dart around the room, but she begins her talk. She fiddles with short dreads that frame her cherubic face. "I am happy that my bipolar daughter is taking her medication. She's really following through on the treatment plan she received from her doctor. We were concerned that her quality of life would remain stagnant, but she signed up for classes at the local college. She can't live on campus, but we are working together as a family to see that she's taken care of."

The others applaud and so do I.

The good news bolsters Houston. His strong voice adds to the celebration. "We found my brother, Mac, living in Seattle. Last month, I told y'all he had been missing the last three years. He comes to Georgia, gets on a good routine with his doctors and medication, and the minute he's stable, he thinks he can do it on his own and disappears. Every call we get, we think it will be a call saying he's dead. I know it's a blessing he'll be home for Christmas. If we could figure out a way to keep him stable this time, I'd be happy."

Delores pipes in. "Is Mac open to seeing a psychologist?"

"He had a psychiatrist last time."

"No. A psychiatrist prescribes medications and treatment plans; a psychologist is the couch-coaxer. Someone Mac can utilize for personal and group therapy."

"I'll check into it. I love my brother and I'm tired of these disappearing acts."

Rita bows out of the conversation. She pushes the huge dark shades she wears closer to her eyes.

"Are you sure?" Delores asks.

"Ain't been no change since the last time. I don't wanna keep saying the same thing over and over again." She stopped, swallowed hard, and continued. "I feel like a failure is all I'm tryna say."

"We may hear something different this time," Delores says.

Rita dawdles. She pulls on her sweater and runs her fingers through her hair. "I want to have my husband committed, but I can't do it. I can't bring myself to lock him away." She rocks a bit and stops. "When he was in good mental health, he was a wonderful man. He was a good provider, he helped with the children, and he was a pro around the house with fixing things. He used to make these model ships with his hands. I should have been watching him more, but his mind slipped away before I could help him, and now me and the children feel stuck."

"Do you try to do any activities with him?" Delores asks.

"He won't leave the house."

"Does family come around?"

"Only immediate. By that, I mean me and the children. The others have fallen by the wayside."

"Before you leave, I have some information I'd like to give you, Rita. Don't give up yet."

Houston chimes in. "Don't give up hope too soon. Every time I see Mac, I feel like anything is possible."

Rita, Carlotta, and Houston look in my direction. They are strangers, but I feel safe with them. "I'm a liar and a fraud." The statement is not for shock value, only the truth.

"What you mean by that, Susan?" Rita asks.

"I went to live with relatives in Atlanta when I was little because of my mother's mental illness. I got into the habit of telling people she was dead. I was embarrassed by the fact I didn't have a normal family like the other kids. It's only now that I'm learning she isn't the only one in the family with schizophrenia. I could have helped her if I hadn't been given away."

"Hold on, now," Rita admonishes. "Speaking from the voice of someone knee-deep in it, sounds like your family was trying to spare you some heartache. Caring for Glenn is a twenty-four-seven job. I don't get a break. Even if I step away, I'm worried about him and fret if he's going to be okay."

For the first time, I consider May and Ray's role in helping my mother. She is not their blood relative, yet they've stuck by her twenty-three years. Visitation, money, clothes, nursing her back to health through episodes.

"Rita, I didn't realize how hard taking care of the mentally ill is until I brought my mother home last month. We weren't in the house two weeks and she attacked me. She said she'd been taking meds and she wasn't."

"Glenn won't take medication, and the sad part about the rules is we can't do anything unless he's a threat to us or himself."

I've complained about her medication and didn't realize even the injections are a blessing.

Delores corrals us back to the meeting. "There are so many people in need around us. If we don't discuss the issues, we can't help each other."

"Susan, I want to talk with you after the meeting if that's okay," Rita says.

We continue chatting until Delores realizes we've gone past our allotted meeting time. She adjourns the meeting and we gather at the snack table.

"It's good to meet you, Susan," Houston says. "You remind me of my daughter."

"It was nice meeting all of you as well."

Rita polishes off two cheese straws and puts a cupcake in a clear container from the table. She asks if it's okay to walk me to my car. I tell everyone goodbye and promise to come back to next month's meeting. I get to the door and Delores calls me.

"Susan, you forgot your gift."

She gets a bag from the table and hands it to me. "Merry Christmas."

I didn't expect camaraderie or a gift, but I'm touched. Rita and I walk outside.

"I wish Jim was back," she says. "I can always count on him for a smoke."

"I can't help you, lady. Ms. Susan is smoke-free."

"Oh, my real name is Jackie Montgomery."

"Toni Williamson."

"Do you have a pen?"

I rifle through my purse for a pen and pad and give it to her. She jots her number down.

"I know you're busy like I am, but if you get the chance, call me sometimes. Maybe I can find out how to help Glenn."

"I'll call you, Jackie."

She opens my door for me. I start the car and chuckle.

"What?"

"Won't get too far on less than half a tank of gas," I say.

"Gas station's two blocks over. You better fill up."

I drive away, glad I took a chance on something different. I have one more month left before I make a decision. If I learn more, Mama will be with me for the long haul.

Chapter 28

I pull alongside a pump at Shell and do a double-take. The dangling "S" on the side of the truck is familiar. *Can't be. Not now and not here.* It is dark, but Evan's truck is next to the air pump. I pump my gas and get out and walk toward his vehicle, startling him with a hello.

"Evan?"

He does a quick glance in my direction and smiles. "What are you doing here?"

"Getting gas."

"Wait a sec until I fill my tire."

He fills his tire and heads over. His clothes are dirty and paint-stained. He flashes his smile again and I remember he is a twin. *Evan. His name is Evan, not Ethan.*

"Hard day at work?"

"Worked on a historic home a few blocks over today."

"Those are the best."

"How would you know?"

"I dabble with houses every now and then."

"I wondered if I'd ever see you again. I've thought about you, but figured you weren't interested since you never called. I even asked Ethan about you, but he told me to drop it. That you had a lot on your plate."

"Hey, that Hermès statement I made is true. And I don't have one plate; I have three."

"We all have baggage." He looks askance at me. "You said you stopped for gas. You drove all the way to the 'Ville for gas?"

"I had…" I pause. I don't know this stranger well enough to tell him what's going on with me. Then again, I shared family history with a house of strangers less than thirty minutes ago.

"It's a little late. Is there somewhere we can go to talk?"

"How about my house?"

My poker face fails me. I scrunch my face at the notion, but he clears the air.

"I'm filthy. I have to take a shower. This is a tad bit later than I normally eat, but I can take you to grab a quick bite or I can cook something for you."

"What about your son?"

"Rhoda has physical custody of him. He stays with me on the weekends."

"No drama, right?"

"Who have you been dating?"

"About that baggage thing. Until June, I'd been with the same man five years. I've heard dating horror stories from my friends."

"Pull out your cell phone."

"Why?"

"Draft a text message to one family member and one friend."

I accept the dare, compose a group text to Willa, Aunt Mavis, and Jordan, and hand him the phone. He types a message. When he's done, he lets me proof the message. *I am with Evan Sutton at 9407 Beehive Lane. His number is 478-555-3297. If something happens to me, alert authorities immediately.*

"Evan?"

"I'm a grown man. I don't have time for games and tricks. Hit send on the message and follow me."

A take-charge man. I like it. I follow him home. The drive is about fifteen minutes, and we pull into a subdivision on Beehive Lane. He parks in his garage and I stay in the driveway. I brace myself for a filthy bachelor pad. He opens the front door and I'm shocked. With the exception of laundry neatly folded on the couch, his house is clean.

"Be back in fifteen."

I turn on the television and flip channels. This is the second adventurous move I've made tonight. I've never been to a man's house after meeting him for a second time. Common sense jolts me, and I place the remote back on the coffee table so I can leave. *This is your last night of freedom before your mother returns. Enjoy it.*

I relax again and flip the channels. If we do nothing else, I can at least get a quick meal. My nerves are too frayed for a sit-down meal, and I'd much rather enjoy some company before Mama comes home tomorrow.

Evan's body odor sways me with Irish Spring. He's cleaned up well. The dome is shining and his muscles bulge in the sweater he wears. I've never been a fan of cowboy boots, but my, they round out his nice body in those jeans.

"You decided what you want to eat?"

"I'm tired. If you worked on a historic home, I'm sure you're tired, too. Let's compromise and order takeout. Dutch."

He's stern and emphatic as he removes a credit card from his wallet. "I can pay for the food."

"You're hosting me, so the least I can do is go half on something to eat. Better yet, let me get this meal since I barged in on you."

"You didn't barge; the pleasure's all mine."

Evan brings out a takeout menu organizer, and we scroll through it for food. I haven't had pizza in ages, so I suggest Mellow Mushroom pizza. Thirty minutes later, we sit at his kitchen table and gorge on Funky Q Chicken and Kosmic Karma pizzas. He wipes sauce from my mouth and we swap life stories.

"You were about to tell me why you're in the 'Ville."

All the lies of omission I shared with Lamonte rush back. I hear the new leaf turning.

"I attended a support group meeting."

He drops his pizza slice on a plate. "I didn't know you were battling addiction."

"I'm not. It was a meeting for family members of the mentally ill. My mother lives with schizophrenia." I wait for him to ask me to leave. When he doesn't, I set a mental timer to see how long it will take for the other shoe to drop.

"Are you her only caretaker?"

"I stepped in to help—" *The truth shall set you free.* "That's a lie. I lived in Atlanta for years and pretended my mother was dead. The *AJC*—"

"Ran the GMH stories. So that was you, well, your mother's story?"

I knock my chair over and grab my purse from the sofa. This was a bad idea. I should have followed my instincts, gassed up, and went home. I race to leave, but Evan blocks the front door, takes my hand, and leads me back inside.

"Why are you running off? I wasn't condemning you. I admire the fact you're here now. A lot of people would have kept the lie going and never came home."

"I probably would have if Lamonte hadn't dumped me and my contracts hadn't dried up."

"But you're home. And your mother is still alive. Move forward."

Evan kneads my hands and leads me back to the sofa. He turns the television off and we sit in silence. Twice in one night, the kindness of strangers has soothed my drained spirit.

Chapter 29

I stir to the smell of coffee and bacon. Aunt Mavis must have let herself in to start breakfast for us. Whiplash isn't engaged in her usual lick fest, so she's probably home with Uncle Ray. I toss in bed and tumble to the floor. This is not my bed or my duvet cover. As a matter of fact, I'm on the floor in front of a sofa. I adjust my eyes to Evan's living room, television, and remote.

"Evan!"

"Yes," he answers.

Enraged, I wrap myself in the duvet cover, grateful that I'm fully clothed. I drag myself to the kitchen where he's thawing out hash browns on the counter. I lift the bag of Ore Idas. These are my favorites.

"The bacon is done. Do you want a cup of coffee?"

"What happened last night? What am I still doing here?"

"You fell asleep. You went out like a light before the news came on. I offered to drive you home and you said no." He closes one eye and says, "This is how you looked on the sofa after I turned the television off."

"I didn't."

"You did."

"What else did I do?"

"I asked what you ate for breakfast and you said Potatoes O'Brien, bacon, and fresh-squeezed juice. You didn't toss at all when I snuck past you to go to the grocery store." He eyes his watch. "I have to be at work in an hour, so the juice is a no-go. Hope you like coffee."

Teasing Willa and Aunt Mavis about drinking coffee has come back to haunt me. "Evan, you didn't have to do any of this for me. I would have gone home last night."

"Both of us were tired. It made no sense for you to leave."

Before I can ask him anything, he points to a facecloth, towel, soap, and a toothbrush on the coffee table. "You can use the guest bathroom to wash up."

I don't feel like a slut, but I do feel foolish for falling asleep in the house of a man I barely know. What if he'd taken advantage of me? What explanation could I have given authorities? "Officer, this fine man whose twin brother I've been lusting after let me come home with him on our first date. I told him I don't usually do this, but one thing led to another."

Do people even do this in this day and time? I jump in the shower and scrub away the feelings I have. I'm smitten with Evan and I don't know how to proceed. I shake away the thoughts. Mama is my priority and there's no room for a man in my life right now. I wrap the towel around myself, tiptoe to the door, and stick my head out.

"Evan?"

I hear his steps near the guest bedroom door. "Do you need anything else?"

"Get my keys from the coffee table and bring the purple travel bag from my trunk."

Clay believes a real woman never travels without extra clothes, especially underwear. When I turned fifteen, he purchased me a pink drawstring bag and hand-painted "spare pair" on the front. I carry it with me to this day.

I hear the thud of my bag outside the door. Evan leaves it and heads to the kitchen. I lotion up and dress in a hurry so we can chat before going our separate ways.

Why can't we spend the day together? The food is delicious and he's even more handsome now that I see him in his surroundings.

"Encore tonight?"

"Evan, I don't think that's a good idea. My mother had an episode and has been staying with my aunt. She comes back home today."

"Last night of freedom?"

"What?"

"You said 'last night of freedom' before you fell asleep."

Now I probably sound like Mama's a burden. "I didn't mean—"

"After our discussion last night, I realized I'd be low on your priority list. I would never put demands on your time in your current situation."

"Thanks, Evan."

"You know how to reach me. I work a lot, but I'm willing to carve out time to get to know you better."

Before he leaves for work, I insist on doing the dishes. It's the least I can do for his generosity. He walks me to my car and puts my bag in the trunk. He hugs me and gives me a forehead peck. I want more but keep my desires at bay. I don't want to give him the wrong impression, and I want to keep the door of friendship open with him.

I head home, tingling from head to toe. Six months ago, Lamonte Dunlap, Jr. was the only man I imagined loving. I don't know much about Evan, but Clay's declaration of love for Russ comes to mind. He said, "Some people you meet; some people you recognize." There is good in Evan, and I recognize it.

I pull into the driveway and my message alert tings. I open Evan's message.

Thanks for trusting me.

I cradle my phone, cheesing harder than I have in a long time.

Chapter 30

We travel in separate vehicles to the annual Christmas Eve service at St. John's. The church grounds are filled to capacity. I am with Willa and her family; Mama is behind us with May and Ray. Whiplash is on punishment for swallowing a sock and a thong. She threw up the thong and passed the sock, thanks to the vet. We get out and are greeted by several members of the church. Mrs. Creasy Taylor saunters over to Willa and me.

"I was hoping you girls would stop by and see me sometimes."

"I'm here for the rest of the holiday season, so we'll try to get by and see you."

"Do that, okay."

We walk toward the church and Cousin Edwina waves to us. Mama catches up with me and flashes her day-of-the-week pill container. "I've been taking my medication, Gumdrop. I don't want to let you down anymore."

"I'm proud of you. I'm with you every step of the way. Willa is, too."

"I know."

Mama's eyes veer to the churchyard graves. Our family is buried here, and for years we placed flowers on our loved ones' tombs. She taps my shoulder. "I'm going to look at Mama's grave before I come inside."

"I'll save a seat for you. I think Aunt Mavis put flowers on Grandma Rose's grave two weeks ago." She follows the trail to her mother.

An announcement board sits to the left of the church. I spy the names of family members who served for years in different capacities at St. John's. Lamonte and I attended a megachurch in Atlanta. I enjoyed the magnificent building and the large crowd, but nothing beats the warmth of a small church where everyone knew each other. "St. John's A.M.E." stands out in large block letters. If Clay could perch on my shoulder like a bird, he'd whisper in my ear, "Honey, they know A.M.E. doesn't stand for African Methodist Episcopal. It means Always Meddling in Everything." I shake off his old saying and head into the church with my family.

Pastor and Sister Wilcox and other church members greet us in the vestibule. They have aged well. He is as distinguished now as he was when I was a child. A squat man with a penchant for fire-and-brimstone sermons, he brought the house down Sunday after Sunday. He'd snatch the microphone from the stand and glide from one end of the stage to the other, swerving in his robe, and stomping his spit-shined 'gators until someone caught the spirit. Ushers rushed to the aide of the slain-in-the-spirit with smelling salts and hand fans. Before I moved, he'd switched his delivery style from whooping to teaching. He told Uncle Raymond running around the church and swinging from the chandeliers didn't count if your walk didn't reflect God's word. Membership shrank, but the faithful embraced his teaching style.

"Seeing you again is like a breath of fresh air, Sister Toni," he says.

"It's good to be home."

He speaks to us individually, praising us for being together again. Sister Wilcox points to the first two pews on the right aisle. "Those are your pews."

We head to the front of the church, and two signs are taped to the pews on either side.

RESERVED: WILLIAMSON.

We shuffle into the seats, one by one. Mama sits on the front pew and asks me to sit with her. Willa and McKenna sit with us as everyone else sits on the second row. The church is decorated for the season with a beautiful white Christmas tree in the corner. The podium is draped in a red velvet cloth and a green-and-gold wreath. Poinsettias line the altar. Pastor Wilcox joins the other men and one woman in the pulpit as the choir livens the church with "Carol of the Bells."

Mama is transfixed and sways in time with the music. Three songs and a prayer later, she moves closer to me. Aunt Mavis confirmed she's taken her meds, but something about her face is distant. The pianist's key tickling fades, and Pastor Wilcox walks to the pulpit.

"I'm passing the baton tonight to Pastor Jared Smith. I've preached the Christmas Eve sermon for years, but tonight, I believe Pastor Smith is gonna take us higher. Amen."

We applaud and the younger man takes the stage. He hoists his Bible on the podium and leans toward us. "Oh, magnify the Lord with me," he says, as the pianist keys up praise break music. Pastor Smith dances side to side and twirls once. He removes a handkerchief from his back pocket and wipes his sweatless forehead.

"Saints, it's good to be with you again."

"Amen," we respond in unison.

"I know your Christmas dinner is simmering for tomorrow's get-together, so I'm going to unpack this message and send you all home." A few laughs rise from the crowd. "Christmas messages always focus on Jesus, the wise men, and livestock. But tonight, I'm going in a different direction. I want the saints to be set free."

"Amen."

"Turn with me to Mark five: one through thirteen and stand for the reading of God's word."

We stand and read with him. As he reads, I'm drawn back to a time when Pastor and Sister Wilcox came to our house. The image of a sick man cutting himself near the tombs plays in my head. There were demons inside him, and they were named Legion. The scripture, the image, the condemnation of the man's illness comes into play for me.

Mama's attention is rapt and discomfort rises in me. Her eyes are as sparkly as two copper pennies as the pastor speaks.

"You may be seated. Today, I want to preach from the subject, Dismissing the Legion in Your Life."

For the next forty-minutes, he browbeats us with a sermon about mental illness. Surely, Pastor Wilcox would not have set us up this way. My stomach sours as Pastor Smith steps out of the pulpit with his cordless microphone and stands center stage.

"How many people do you know rely on medication instead of the Lord?"

Incredulous, Willa and I look at each other. I tear the program bulletin in half and scribble on the white lines, *What the hell? You have to be kidding me!*

"Pharmaceutical companies are cleaning up off the ignorance of the world. Prozac for this. Lexapro for that. When was the last time you fell down on your knees and asked Jesus to cure you?"

Mama shoots up. "Hallelujah!"

"He is a balm in Gilead, the Great I am, Master, Ruler, Healer. What better way is there than the Truth? The Light?" His back dips after he says "The Light."

I turn around as Aunt Mavis excuses herself from the service. Uncle Raymond trails her. Mama's feet are planted to the floor. With each declaration Pastor Smith spews, her eyes grow wider and her arms give him permission to continue. "Preach, Reverend, Preach!" she yells.

"Imagine the demon-possessed man at the tombs cutting himself, crying out for help and all those voices inside him competing for his attention."

"Yes, Lord!"

I hold my stomach and lurch forward. *Be strong for Mama.* I sit back, praying he wraps this sermon up before I sneak into the choir stand and unplug the audio equipment. Pastor Wilcox averts his eyes. I search the church for Sister Wilcox. She is equally complicit as she quickly looks away when our eyes meet.

The congregation eggs him on. He comes out into the center aisle and paces up and down with the microphone.

"Come out, Legion!"

Members stand. Some are slain in the spirit; others speak in tongues. Pastor Smith takes backward steps and stands in the center of the floor behind the altar.

"Quickly, quickly, if you know a Legion is holding you down, don't walk; run to the altar right now! I want to pray for you."

Several people dash toward the altar and fall to their knees. Some lay prostrate, crying, screaming, begging to be rid of their demons. Pastor Smith has his arms around Mama and his hands on her forehead. He speaks words over her as Willa and I rise to rescue our mother. Two men block our path as Pastor Smith gives her head a shove. She falls back into the men's arms. They carry her back to her seat as two ushers fan her on either side. Pastor Smith lays hands on bowed heads around the altar and continues to yell, "Legion, come out! Legion, come out!"

Sister Wilcox mouths a command to a woman in the choir stand, who stands amid the chaos. The pianist slides on the organ bench and cues up a Mahalia Jackson tune. Willa and I give each other a cryptic look again when the first verse of "Move On Up a Little Higher" starts.

Mama plops down. "I knew Jesus and 'Halia would give me an answer."

She takes a seat near the choir stand, where the soloist manipulates the lyrics with her rich voice. She holds the phrase "soon one morning" as if she's in a vocal contest. She sings "coming over hills and mountains" and coaxes Mama to come into the choir stand to sing. Someone gives her a microphone, and she sings the best she can, her fractured voice limping along with the soloist's pristine sound. Pleased with themselves, Sister Wilcox joins her husband in the pulpit and they both pat Pastor Smith's back. Mama is back in her far-off land as she sings, "Howdy howdy, and never goodbye."

Chapter 31

Nothingness awakens me. No grits, eggs, or the smell of Mama's seasoned fish. Dinner is at May and Ray's today. Bringing Mama from church last night was like trying to con a resting angel off a cloud, darn near impossible. She repeated the phrase, "I've got the answer," over and over. Aunt Mavis injected Haldol to calm her nerves, but the high from church lingered for hours. I put her in bed with me and made sure she was comfortable. Her side of the bed is empty now. It's early, but I'll get up and make breakfast. She has cooked three mornings, and I will attempt something for us today. Her Christmas gift is still in the trunk of my car. I could stay in bed all day and skip Christmas after last night.

"Mama."

Her Christmas dinner outfit hangs on the closet door. The matching jewelry set sparkles in the sunlight. I promised Mama I'd do big curls for her today since the rinse took well.

"Mama!"

I put on my robe and slippers. "Mama. Let's get ready before I crawl back in bed for the rest of the holiday season."

I head toward the living room. When we were younger, she'd sneak peeks at the gifts Daddy bought her. My heart drops. The front door is wide open and I feel cold December air.

"Mama!"

She isn't in the living room. I run to the porch. It is empty. I search the yard with no luck. I am yelling at the top of my lungs for her. I unzip my rob pocket for my phone and dial my aunt.

"Is Mama there?"

"No."

Panic fills my voice. "Aunt Mavis, she's gone! I've checked all the rooms, outside, she's not here."

"How long has she been missing?"

"She was in bed when I used the bathroom this morning at three."

"We're heading there now."

If something happens to her, I'll never forgive myself. Her shoes are next to the bed. I search her chest of drawers to see if she wore something different than her gown. Her clothes are neatly folded and stacked, and nothing new has been touched. I sift through each drawer and come up with clothing. The bottom drawer contains random items I haven't seen in years—an old answering machine, lesson plans from her teaching years, and a dusty Polaroid camera.

A Tampa Nugget cigar box captures my attention. Photos, post-cards, and maps fill the box. A folded sheet of paper has hearts and circles drawn on it. I open the paper to Mama's writing. Each sentence is printed in her fancy cursive writing. *They love me. They hate me. They want me to die. I want to die. Paul. Willa. Toni.* The sentences are written in three rows and fill the sheet. I fold the paper again and put it back in the box.

I shower as fast as I can and get dressed. I barely tie my shoestrings when I hear a horn blowing in the front yard. I race out and jump inside Don's vehicle. There is lots of space, but tension fills the vehicle.

Uncle Ray's anger spills over from last night. "I can't believe Wilcox was so cruel."

Aunt Mavis nods. "I'd rather they didn't invite us at all instead of humiliating her."

Don speeds up and addresses us. "Where do you want me to drive?"

Willa is frantic and responds as if Don only asked her the question. "She hasn't been gone twenty-four hours, so we can't report her as a missing person."

I want to demand he drive to the Wilcoxes, but I say, "Let's ride around here first, then we'll go downtown."

The drive takes us around backroads, side alleys, and abandoned houses. Don drives to the church again, looking for clues. We get out, walk around the graves, and find nothing.

"I know it's Christmas, but call the sheriff anyway. She couldn't have gotten too far on foot," Uncle Raymond says.

I wait for Uncle Raymond to dial the sheriff before I sneak around the corner to place a call. I make sure no one sees me and dial.

"Merry Christmas, Crittenden residence."

"Cousin Edwina, Mama's missing."

"I'm not surprised after that trick Wilcox pulled last night. Where are you now?"

"We came back to the church to see if she's here. She's wearing a gown and maybe some slippers. I looked in the closet and her coats are all there."

"Lord have mercy!"

"Do you know where she might be?"

Cousin Edwina fumbles with something and I hear her say, "Walt, let's get up so we can help find Greta."

"Cousin Edwina, I didn't mean to disturb you. I only wanted to find out if she went anywhere special when she was sad."

"We're family. No way I'm gonna sit here and not help you find Greta. You said you all are at the church?"

"Yes, ma'am."

"Let me see who else I can round up and I'll call you back."

I place my phone back in my pocket before Aunt Mavis and Willa see me. Willa and McKenna come around the corner to comfort me while Uncle Ray dials someone.

"Are you okay, Toni?" Willa asks.

"No. I've been nothing but trouble for Mama since I came back. She was better off at GMH before I stirred up the pot and tried to bring her home."

"Stop blaming yourself. She longed for a reunion with us and she got it."

"At what cost?"

"At the cost of you seeing what the family tried to shield both of us from so many years ago. Toni, Mama is sick. She will always be schizophrenic. Medicine, psychotherapy, and other things will help, but she will always need attention and constant care."

"She needs us, Willa."

"She needs a team of people to support her. You can't do it alone."

"Let's drive by the house again," Uncle Raymond says. "She might have come back."

We pile into Don's vehicle again and ride to the home-house in silence. Cousin Edwina's call interrupts my train of thought.

"I called a few people and they're meeting at Golden Pantry. If you all will head this way, we can pull together a search party and divide up in parts of the county."

"Thanks, Edwina. I'll let everyone know."

"Was that Edwina Crittenden?" Aunt Mavis asks.

"Yes."

"What does she want?"

I swallow hard and respond, "I called her and asked if she could help us find Mama."

Aunt Mavis's irritation is evident. She scoots away from Uncle Raymond and looks out the window.

"Doesn't it make sense for someone to be home in case Mama comes back? Cousin Edwina has people meeting at Golden Pantry. Meet her there and I can stay at the house."

St. John's is not far from our home. "Call me as soon as you hear something," I say as I exit the SUV.

Willa pulls on her door to come inside with me, but I shake my head. I want to be alone.

Chapter 32

Greta

Nothing beats the feeling of Jesus giving you the answers you need. I knew something wasn't right about having all that medication in my system. I kept praying to Jesus, asking him what he wanted me to do. When we were at the concert, he turned his back on me. I was being disobedient when I told him I would keep his commandments and didn't. It is time I follow my heart and do the right thing. I've been lonely without Jesus and 'Halia. Come to think of it, they've been with me longer than I've been with my husband and children. Makes no sense for me to pretend it's been an easy ride since I saw the girls again. This dream I had about them running to me and picking back up where we left off didn't go so well.

Toni probably wouldn't have come to see me if her picture wasn't in the paper. She won't say it, but if that Lamonte character told her to come back to him tomorrow, I believe she'd go. It's that way with the Williamson women. My mother, Rose, loved my daddy, Horace. Love wasn't enough to keep them together. He left her because she was sick like I am. It's bad enough the men leave, but it's hard when friends leave you too.

Mavis doesn't know about this, but I want to tell it anyway. A couple days ago, I went to my follow-up visit. After the follow-up, we went to the community center for bingo. Well, it was supposed to be bingo. The regular lady who comes was sick, and this artsy, twenty-something girl was there. I'm talking a real kook. I had my heart set on playing bingo, and she goes to the chalkboard in the room and writes some things down. Little silly exercises like how many gumballs are in this jar? What was the best vacation you ever took? Who is the nicest person you've ever met? She told us to stick with her because she was warming us up for the exercise of the day. About fifteen minutes later, she went around the room and gave everyone a legal pad and pens. We were given twenty minutes to write freestyle. Poem, essay, short story, didn't matter. We had twenty minutes to put our thoughts down on paper. Since Jesus and 'Halia hadn't been to see me in a long time, I asked them to come get me for good. I promised Jesus I would follow his commandments, and I promised 'Halia I'd help her in the heavenly choir. I wrote those words so fast my heart was pounding. When I got to the end of my paper, I asked Jesus to give me a sign within seventy-two hours. If a mental facility can make me stay against my will for a seventy-two-hour hold, I figure Jesus can tell me what to do about this situation of being lonely. Of going in and out of GMH. Of being misunderstood by everybody.

Wouldn't you know it, he gave me all the signs and wonders in church. Christmas Eve service wasn't ordinary this year. Truth be told, I had gotten tired of Wilcox since he stopped all the fire and brimstone. Teaching in the pulpit is all right, but it's good to have a pastor to release the fire shut up in your bones. Pastor Smith was Jesus's messenger. He gave me the answer I needed. From his choice of scripture, to his Legion reference, to the young lady singing my favorite song, it's like Jesus timed everything perfectly. They're not going to kick up a big fuss once I'm gone anyway.

I knew last night was nothing but Jesus, since I've never heard anyone talk about the pharmaceutical companies in the pulpit. When Smith got revved up, I saw Toni write something on a piece of paper to Willa. I don't know what she said, but they were acting like they didn't empathize with my sickness. I know Willa doesn't care much for me, but Toni shocked me going against what the pastor said. She's been here from Atlanta long enough to see what those pills and the shots do to me. For her to sit there and not have compassion broke my heart but made me realize it's time to let them go. This won't be so hard. Won't be hard at all.

Good to know prayers are still answered. I found the perfect place to lay my burdens down. No one has to worry about me anymore. Maybe they'll find me, maybe they won't.

Now that I'm following His commandments again, I'm waiting for Jesus and 'Halia to stop by and pick me up. I wonder if it will be in a chariot or a regular car. They should be able to see me where I am. I have my feet kicked up where Jesus told me to be, and I see birds flying overhead. I need something to cover me up to keep me warm, but I have to trust the two of them to do that for me, too.

Chapter 33

Willa texts a picture of the crowd gathered at Golden Pantry. I am moved by the number of people who stand with my family, who've given up their Christmas morning to search for Mama. I look at the picture closely and see Cousin Edwina and Ms. Creasy Taylor. My phone trills. Jordan's calling. I let it go to voicemail, but she calls again. I answer with no holiday spirit.

"Merry Christmas, *bon ami!*"

I say nothing and contemplate hanging up. I have no spirit, no cheer.

"Toni, what's wrong?"

The sniffles turn crying. I lean on the bed and smell where she lay a few hours ago. Her distinct body odor clings to the sheets and pillows.

"Calm down and tell me what's going on," Jordan says. I picture her glowing face and the baby bump. My chaos and confusion shouldn't interrupt her holiday.

"I can't talk about it right now, Jordan."

"Toni, you slipped away from me once with this evasiveness. I am your friend and I love you. I don't care about your past. I'm here for you. Talk to me."

"Mama's missing."

"When did this happen?"

"This morning."

She is silent. I wait for her to speak. "I can be there in two hours."

"No. It's Christmas. I don't want you traveling today. Stay where you are and let me keep you posted."

"Had she been taking her medication?"

"Yes. We went to church last night and were ambushed with a sermon about mental illness. I'm positive Pastor Wilcox did it on purpose."

"On purpose, as in…?"

"As in a younger pastor took the pulpit and said all the mentally ill need is God, not meds. Mama took to the message with so much joy and delight it frightened us."

"That's terrible. What are you all planning to do about his antics?"

"I want to find her. We'll deal with him later."

"Does anyone suspect her whereabouts? Does she go to a particular place when she's sad?"

"A search party has gathered in town, and I'm waiting here in case she comes back. I'm trying not to panic or think the worst."

"My offer stands. I can be there in two hours."

"I'd love that, Jordan. If it's no trouble."

"I'm on the road again. See you soon."

I put my coat on and walk the yard again. Maybe there is somewhere I haven't explored. Secret spots and escape routes fill the yard. If she is sitting alone and gathering thoughts, I'd be pleased. I just want to see her again. I search the well again. The concrete top remains, but the bucket has been moved. I follow a trail in back of the well and find nothing. Antsy, I grab my keys, lock the house, and head to Golden Pantry. I'll go crazy waiting around the house.

The crowd huddles in mini groups at Golden Pantry. A bulky man disseminates information. He gives instructions to each group as he speaks with a bullhorn.

Aunt Mavis flags me as I park. "Did she come back to the house?"

"Not yet. I got tired of waiting there and decided to come here."

"Willa, Don, and McKenna joined a group of people on the Augusta Highway. Jack Morris is passing out directions to a few other locations in town she may have wandered off."

"Where are you going to search for her?" I ask.

"I'm waiting for Jack to assign a new location."

"Aunt Mavis, may I speak to you in my car?"

She follows me and we sit. "I'm going back to Atlanta after Mama's found. No matter the outcome, I realize I don't belong here. I've caused her nothing but trouble since I got here."

"She's glad you're here. If you leave, it will crush her."

"If I leave, she can get back to her old routine. I've upended her."

"You've only been here a few months. You need to give her at least a year to adjust to you being here for her. It's a little bumpy, but you'll get used to caring for her."

"This discharge has been a burden I don't want to bear."

Aunt Mavis clenches and unclenches her fists. I flinch when she raises her hand, but she doesn't hit me. Instead, she clutches the passenger door. "A burden *you* don't want to bear? Who do you think has been bearing the burden for her care since you've been away?"

"Aunt Mavis…"

"Don't Aunt Mavis me! Ray is right. You've used what we did as an excuse to be selfish and deny you have family. Bad enough you lived that close to us and never once tried to visit your own mother."

I hold her arm, but she frees herself from my grip and goes back to her mini group. She whispers something to Ray and he shakes his head. I start my engine so I can go back home and wait for Jordan to arrive. There's time for me to pack and get on the road to Atlanta. My damage is done in Sparta.

I don't make it out of the parking lot before a commotion ensues. Aunt Mavis flags me again. "You can't leave right now, Toni. They found Greta."

Chapter 34

We arrive at Dobson's Farm in Springfield. A massive, brick ranch sits in front of a fish pond and livestock holding pens. A sign in front of the farm advertises chickens, cows, goats and pigs for sale. A yellow storage unit with painted black bees and a large honey jar is nestled on the right side of the farm. The sign above the bees reads "The Honey Hole." An ambulance whizzes past us and drives in back of the farm. I am vaguely familiar with this place. The greater mystery is how Mama got this far from where we live. On foot, this would have taken her at least two hours to walk.

A man wielding a shovel over his shoulders approaches us. Although the five of us and Whiplash stand together, several people from the search drove to the farm as well.

"That's Andie Dobson," Aunt Mavis whispers to us. "Been knowing us, especially your uncle, for years."

Mr. Dobson looks like he's skipping Christmas too. His overalls and hat have mud stains. He pulls a pair of gloves from his pocket and slips them on. He takes Uncle Ray's hand as a peace offering instead of a handshake.

"Ray."

"Where is she, Andie?"

He points in back of the house toward the holding pens. He leads us toward the pigs. I don't want to see my mother's dead body. I want to remember her as she was in the church.

"How long has she…" My voice trails off as I address Mr. Dobson. Whiplash yips but isn't barking as she usually does.

"How long has she what?"

Willa takes my hand and picks up the conversation. "We don't want to see her dead."

Mr. Dobson scratches his head beneath his Dobson Farms cap. "She's not dead. She's being stubborn, that's what she is."

I blink several times, unsure if I heard him correctly. "She's not?"

"Darndest thing. I did a run to Crawfordsville yesterday to deliver two cows and my last five pigs. Got a pretty penny for all of 'em. I woke up this morning to some noises but ignored it. My nephews double as my farm help, so I thought they were playing their radio and being silly. I tossed and turned because the noise wouldn't stop. About forty minutes ago, I crept back to the hog troughs and there she was, laying in repose. I thought she was dead until I saw her chest rising and falling." He turns to Uncle Ray. "I been knowing y'all for years, but she damned near scared the life outta me." He wipes his forehead with his gloved hands.

Uncle Ray moves closer. "Did she say anything?"

"She said the Lord and somebody else was coming to pick her up after the legion got out of her body. Said something about keeping commandments. She babbled on and on from subject to subject but would never let me move her."

The five of us head back to the pens in time to see the paramedics lifting her body from a trough. She is kicking and screaming, saying Jesus and 'Halia spoke through the pastor. She says her demons will go into pigs and she will be free again. Some members of the search team gawk; others turn away.

"Who's riding with us?" the paramedic asks.

Everyone looks at me. I climb in back of the ambulance with my mother. Although the paramedics cover her body with a sheet, the bottom of her gown shows. It is muddy and holds the stench of the animals, as do her dirty feet. She reaches for my hands, but I jerk back. Anger consumes me. I am angrier at the set-up at church instead of my mother, but the circumstances make it difficult to embrace her.

The paramedics ask perfunctory questions as I watch her play an imaginary piano. She bangs the keys as the organist did at church. We arrive at Oconee Regional again. Same ER. Same situation. The rest of the family joins me. We wait for such a long time for them to call us back. A kind nurse brings us coffee and a few snacks from the vending machine. I sip the coffee but pass on the food. Uncle Ray walks Whiplash in the parking lot while we wait for the news.

The same nurse points us out to an on-call doctor, who joins us in the waiting area.

"Family of Greta Williamson?"

"Yes," we say in unison.

He flips a chart. "Mrs. Williamson is no stranger to us here. The inconsistency of her medication has caused another break. The good news is she has requested a voluntary admission to GMH."

Willa holds my hand. "Are you sure?"

"She asked to speak to her daughters. That's why I came down. She's in room three-one-one."

Aunt Mavis, Don, and McKenna give us permission to go with their eyes. We take the elevator, afraid of what Mama will do or say. We enter her room and she is sedate. Her eyes are red, but she smiles at us.

"Come sit down with me." We sit on her bed and take her hands. "I'm out of apologies."

"Mama, it's Christmas. We can talk about this another time. We're glad you're okay. You gave us a scare," I say. For the first time since the ambulance ride, my heart softens toward her.

"I'm sick like my mama and I'm not getting any better. I don't want to keep putting you all through these changes."

Willa speaks for us now. "We all have to give it time."

"I've given it over thirty years, and look at me. I don't have straight thoughts until I'm medicated."

"Things can change," I say.

"Not without me doing things to hurt everybody else. I had my reunion with you two. It's time for me to go back to GMH."

"Mama, the home-house is ready and you still have the job lined up at Ray of Hope."

"If it's for me, it'll be there when I come out for good. For now, I need to go back. Andie almost had a heart attack when he saw me, and I can't erase the memory of being upset about you taking my pills from my pocket."

"I've moved back to help you. Will you give it another shot with me?"

"I don't think so, Gumdrop."

Willa tries to change her mind. "Mama, you have to try a variety of things. You need the meds and therapy. Toni and I will help you."

Mama faces me. "Why, Toni? I understand why Willa didn't want to have anything to do with me. Why did you turn your back on me?"

"There's no particular reason."

"I believe there is."

Willa waits for the answer as well. I refuse to address anything with Mama about our past.

"Toni, whatever it is, I'll rest better knowing how I offended you. The two of you keep talking about being here for me. At least tell me what happened all those years ago. Why did Mavis and Clayton take you away?"

I don't want to do this. Russ and Clay got me past this, and I hate revisiting it. I'm better, thanks to Russ, but it feels awkward.

"Mama." I remove my coat and place it across the chair. I start with the top button and work my way down. When I open my blouse, Willa touches me like Russ touched me at the engagement party.

She traces the cuts on my stomach. "Toni, no," she says.

I face my mother full-on. "I wanted to feel what you felt, Mama, so I created my own pain. I fired up the front unit on the gas oven, warmed up the tip of a knife, and made small cuts at first. Each cut made me feel closer to you. The night before I moved away, Aunt Mavis caught me cutting my stomach. I dropped the knife on the floor, but by then it was too late; I couldn't deny it. The next day, I was riding shotgun with Clay to Atlanta. They had been talking and whispering about a lot of things for a while, saying my dependence on you was too much. That my desire to protect you was unhealthy. When I got to Atlanta, Russ mixed coconut, shea, and tea tree oils and rubbed my stomach for months until it got better. I don't wear bikinis, I've never made love with the lights on, and I avoided PE in high school after a few girls dubbed my stomach Alcatraz wire."

They stare at my stomach before Mama speaks. "I don't feel worthy to have you as my daughters. I don't feel worthy."

I quickly rebutton my blouse, leave the room, and sit in a small waiting area. I vowed never to let Mama see my stomach, my missteps. My message alert tings. Two texts have come in. Jordan wants to know where I am and Evan wishes me Merry Christmas.

I fire off a text of my own.

Aunt Mavis, I'm going to the home-house. I'll stop by later for dinner.

Chapter 35

Jordan's stomach is so big, she looks like she's carrying twins. How else can a belly grow that fast, unless two children are chomping at the bit to get here. I'm careful as I embrace her and invite her inside. She does a slight waddle and sits down on the sofa.

"Mr. Stewart wasn't working today, so I had to find my way back to the home-house by memory. Pregnancy brain is real. I'm already starting to forget things."

"He's not working because he helped with the search for my mom."

She rubs her bundle of joy and takes a deep breath. "How is she?"

"She's fine. She's in the hospital now. When she's discharged, she's voluntarily going back to GMH."

"Voluntarily?"

"Yep, surprised us all."

"I really wanted you to bond with her."

"So did I. I'm considering moving back to Sparta for good to help her out. I've been running for years, and it's time to slow down."

"Where will you live?"

"Here. My dad made sure the house stayed in the family. Where I'll work is a different story."

"Not so fast. I called earlier because I saw an ad." She opens her bag and fans my face with the paperwork. "Reynolds Home-A-Rama is seeking interior designers and architects for their spring show. You have a great portfolio of work. Give it a shot."

"I've been wanting to do a Home-A-Rama for years. Had too much on my plate."

"This gives you an opportunity to showcase your unique style and drum up new clients. Have you tried working since you've been here?"

"No. I miss my clients. Evan told me there are great thrift and decorating stores in this area." Jordan's stomach growls. "Come with me to raid the fridge. Your belly just twerked."

"I know you don't think I'm eating your cooking."

"Why not?"

Her smirk sums up her feelings. "We starved because of your kitchen screw-ups."

"My cooking wasn't that bad."

The second smirk is more severe. "If you give my baby food poisoning, our friendship is done! Kaput."

"I'll make my mother's fish for you. Have a seat at the island." I dress filets and make coleslaw the way Mama showed me last month. Jordan is impressed as she gobbles down the food. We sip mocktails and gorge on Mama's ambrosia. The doorbell startles me.

"Wait here."

I peek through the front window curtains. Aunt Mavis gives a slack wave. She is alone and carries a Bible. I open the door, half-expecting her to report more drama about my mother.

"Come in."

"You have company?"

"My friend, Jordan, drove down from Atlanta. She doesn't know it yet, but she's coming to dinner with me at your place later, and she's spending the night. Come meet her."

Aunt Mavis follows me, but discomfort crowds her face. She is pleasant enough, but something troubles her.

"Aunt Mavis, this is my best friend, Jordan."

"It's nice to meet you. Toni's told me a lot of good things about you. Glad you've been there for my niece all these years."

"Would you like something to eat, Aunt Mavis?"

"No, thank you. We have enough food at the house to feed an army." She scans the kitchen. "I'd like to speak with you in private."

Jordan pours more ambrosia in a bowl as Aunt Mavis leads the way to the living room. I toss a few logs on the fire and sit next to her. She fiddles with the Bible and places it on her lap.

"I was out of line this morning."

"When?"

"When I yelled at you. I had no right to speak to you that way."

"Everyone's nerves were frayed."

"Fear got the best of me. If Greta had died, I wouldn't have the chance to apologize to you or her."

"For?"

Her Bible springs open and she rifles through the scriptures. A Hancock County courthouse envelope is mixed in with newspaper clippings and notices.

"Willa told me about you opening your shirt today. I've tried blocking the image of you cutting yourself all these years. Clay and I had been discussing getting you to safety for a while. When I witnessed you pierce your skin without flinching, I knew you'd been exposed to more than you could handle."

"I figured as much."

"There's more."

"Go on."

She opens the courthouse envelope. The document is musty but spotless. The termination of parental rights form is official and signed by both my parents.

"What does this mean?"

"Look closely."

The document almost fooled me, but the loops tell the story. My mother's "G" was always big and showy. This one misses the mark. My father's "P" was the largest of his letters when he signed documents. I'd sit in his lap and watch him sign everything with his initials, *PMW*, draw a circle around it, and put "OK" at the end.

"You and Clay forged their signatures?"

She nods. "We thought it was the best thing for you."

"Does Daddy know?"

"He was gone before we hatched our plan."

"How were you able to do it?"

"Those are the perks of small-town living. Judge Anderson Taylor helped us with the process. He'd known Greta's people for years and was more than willing to help make sure you didn't suffer the same fate."

"Taylor?"

"He's dead, God rest his soul, but his wife, Creasy, still lives here."

"She asked me and Willa to call her while we were at the Pine Tree Festival."

"She always thought she was right as rain and didn't approve of what we did. She said if she ever saw you again, she'd tell you. Guess I beat her to it."

I hold the document and marvel at how quickly fate can change at the hands of someone else. What would things have been like had I stayed? Had we stayed? Given Mama's erratic behavior, it was only a matter of time before she may have turned on me as well.

"I was deceitful. I've done some underhanded things when it comes to your mother's side of the family, but I wouldn't change a thing if it meant seeing you grow up to be the smart, accomplished woman you've become."

I soak in her words and her sacrifice. I take it all in piece by piece.

Chapter 36

Six Months Later

I smile for the camera with other designers and architects outside Reynolds Home-A-Rama's grand opening. My family, Jordan, and Evan wait for me to finish the photos. Whiplash has found a friend and is chasing butterflies around a tree. Mama chats with Jackie Montgomery from Beacon Cottage. You'd never guess they met two months ago. I break from the crowd to visit my biggest supporters.

"Did you dedicate a room to me and Russ?" Clay asks. Russ moves the wheelchair near the accessibility ramp of the house I decorated. Clay's face has puffed up, and he's put on a few extra pounds.

Everyone else walks the grounds in search of their dream home. Evan walks over to us.

"Clay and Russ, this is my friend, Evan Sutton."

"Pleased to meet you," Clay says. "Toni is the shine in our moon. You have to answer to us if you don't take good care of her."

"Clay, we're just friends."

"Friendship leads to other things. Isn't that right, Russ?"

"Enough, you two. We're taking it one day at a time."

Evan shakes their hands and makes small talk. He was able to get in on the building action with two homes in the subdivision. After he did interior painting and installed hardwood flooring, a few local builders asked if he'd be interested in a few subcontract jobs.

I mouth to him, "Be right back."

Jackie makes Mama laugh again. I'm jealous and want in on the action.

"What are you two laughing about?"

"Jackie doesn't believe you can't cook. I told her your smarts would get you through life."

"I'm getting better and you know it."

"You'd better. That's a handsome man you might have to feed someday."

"We're just friends."

Evan is next to one of the houses smiling at me. We're getting closer, but I'm not ready to take the love plunge. I'm getting to know him slowly, all of him, and he is doing the same with me. He gained two million brownie points the night we were in my yard turning dirt for a garden when Lamonte showed up unannounced. Had the nerve to say he'd made a mistake, couldn't live without me, and wanted me to give him a second chance. I bet ole Stewart told him where I lived. Evan put his arms around me and gave Lamonte the deadliest look. Didn't say a word; just looked at him until he jumped in his ride and drove away.

Willa and her family couldn't make the trip due to McKenna's international meet, but they sent lovely flowers congratulating me on a job well done. Jordan and my godson, Caden, are standing near my favorite model home. I make my way over to them; Caden coos when he sees me.

I take Caden from her arms. "Thank you so much for making this possible. I wouldn't have the job if it weren't for you. "

"You did this! I knew this was your thing when I saw the notice. Watch this job leads to many others."

I sniff Caden's baby powder freshness. I swear if I see one of those baby contests, I'll enter him. He has beautiful dark-brown eyes, curly hair, and a smile that will melt the coldest heart. He's an old soul who's been here before. He's wearing the blue sailor outfit I picked out for him a few weeks ago.

Evan walks toward me and puts his arms around me. Caden giggles at Evan. I steal a quick peck and rub the dome.

"Careful, people are watching."

"So what?"

"You're the one who left the spare pair in my guest bedroom a few months ago. I know you did that on purpose so you could see me again."

"Dream on, man." I hand Caden back to Jordan.

Jackie and Mama inch closer to us. "What time are we leaving?" Mama asks.

"In an hour."

"Will you take me inside so I can take my medication?"

"Sure."

I proudly walk Mama into one of the decorated homes. The builders stocked the fridge with beverages and snacks for the guests. She swipes a Sprite, pops open the tab, and takes a Zyprexa.

We didn't speak for two months after the Christmas Day incident. She wrote me a long letter asking if I'd be willing to give her one more try. She vowed to take her medication and go to therapy. I was skeptical but led with my head instead of my heart this time. I attend Beacon Cottage and NAMI meetings faithfully. Willa joins me when she can. Mama is getting the hang of group therapy, and Aunt Mavis, Uncle Ray, and Cousin Edwina rotate shifts with me when I'm tired.

Evan's friendship has been a godsend. He respects me, surprises me with thoughtful gestures, and is open to learning about my mother's illness. He knows if we get closer, Mama and I are a package deal.

Coming home to stay has been the best thing for me. Daddy's gift of the home-house has enabled me to relax and get my bearings straight. I renewed Giovanna's lease for another year, and I moved most of my Virginia Avenue items to Sparta. The day I decided to come home for good, I consulted my longtime friend, Mr. Juggles. I lifted his head, fished around for a fortune, and read it aloud.

Bloom Where You Are Planted.

That's exactly what I'm doing, and I have Mama to thank for this new life.

Author's Note

This is the book that almost wasn't. After receiving a grant from the Indiana Arts Commission in 2005 to do research at a mental health facility in Milledgeville, GA, I wrote three hundred pages of gobbledygook and gave it to my editor, Robert Coalson. He said he enjoyed the story but argued the story was Toni's, not Greta's. He said her voice was stronger in death than Greta's was in life. In the first manuscript, Toni was a twenty-three-year old who'd died of Lupus. I wrote the second manuscript in Clayton's voice with no luck. I tried the third manuscript from Mavis's point-of-view and it fizzled. I tossed those manuscripts in a drawer and decided to try other genres. I kept reading the mantra, writers write, so I tried my hand at contemporary women's fiction. I was so blessed to land an agent, be published by the magnificent author and movie maven, Zane, and realize my dream of becoming an author. The old crew never left me, though. Toni, Greta, Mavis, and Clayton kept popping up in my mind, telling me what was new with them, how they wanted readers to take them home. Thanks to the person tinkering at the *Indy Star News* copy desk who drew the Duke University coach as a devil, *Wouldn't Change a Thing* was born. The embarrassment felt by the city after the story hit the front page kicked my "what if" into overdrive.

My desire to tell Greta's story was born of my fascination to understand the mind's fragility and my family's struggle with a mentally ill loved one. My childhood and teen years were spent visiting my relative. During visits with her on the hospital grounds, a male patient always found me and greeted me with the question, "Do you know when World War III is coming?" I shrugged. He responded, "May 28, 2050." His hallucinations were of war heroes, namely Napoleon and Custer. He asked me if I could see them having lunch on the grass. I told him yes because he believed they were. Our family was clear: the clandestine visits were not to be shared with others because, "we don't discuss those kinds of things." I hope this story helps someone know you are not alone and help is available.

Thank you, God, for allowing me to see another book in print. I don't take it for granted in the current publishing climate. Thank you Sara, Zane, and Charmaine, for giving me a forum to share this work. Keith Saunders, I well up whenever I see the book cover. Thank you for making our beautiful courthouse immortal with your phenomenal design work. Tuane Hearn of TP Hearn Productions and Matt Hanthorn of Brainstorm Print, thanks for the beautiful promo items.

To my beta readers, Andrea Allen, Jerine Campbell, Devetrice Conyers-Hinton, Author Cathy Jo, and Markina Mapp, your feedback helped me tremendously. Author Renee Swindle, we need to negotiate the price of your impromptu inbox workshop. Without you, this book would not have been completed.

To the lovely book ambassadors who cheer me on, spread the word, and help me through my writing haze: Celestine Allen, Ylana Aukamp, Teresa Beasley, Julia Blues, Ben Burgess, Jr., Tumika Cain, David Campbell, Hulian Campbell, Malik Campbell, Tracy Cooper, Ella Curry, Mary Finley, Tressia Gibbs, Shiera Goff, Yolanda Gore, Latanya Hive, Alvin Horn, Barbara Jo, Joy Jones, Kim Knight, Linnesia Lattimore, Becky Lawrence, Curtis Lawrence,

David Lawrence, Lillie Lawrence, William Lawrence, Jason Lee, Lasheera Lee, Barbara Mapp, Angelia Menchan, Tremayne Moore, Deborah Owsley, Cherlisa Starks-Richardson, Johnathan Royal, Orsayor Simmons, Latrealle Smith, Nicole Scott-Tate, Trisha R. Thomas, Adrienne Thompson, Tiffany Tyler, Kimyatta Walker, Ladonna Wattley, Cyress Webb, and A'ndrea Wilson.

To the New Beginnings Westside crew: Sydney Edmonds, Dawn Jones, and Tammi Kinchlow. Thank you for the love, fellowship, and prayers. You are the epitome of what it means to have sisters in Christ and Titus 2 loving. I'm so glad God allowed our paths to cross.

To the Indiana Arts Commission, thanks for trusting me with research and editing funds. You planted the seed for this book and I'm so grateful. To the staff, doctors, and nurses at Central State Hospital, I heart you for opening your doors to me. For the consumers who shared your stories, triumphs, and defeats, thank you for trusting me with your secrets.

To readers and book clubs, there'd be no Author Stacy Campbell without you. Thank you for the Skype and house meetings, emails, reviews, good food, good conversation, and laugh-out-loud moments. To the Sisters Book Club of Grovetown, Georgia, Coffee and A Good Book Book Club of Augusta, GA, OOSA Book Club of St. Louis, MO, Divas Do Read of Summerville, South Carolina, and Sistah Friends Book Club of Lawrenceville, Georgia, 2014 was so special because of your kindness toward me. The red velvet cake didn't hurt either. ☺

If you know of someone who may need help, or if you need help or want to learn more about mental illness or treatment, contact The National Alliance on Mental Illness (NAMI) at 1-800-950-6264 or www.nami.org.

About the Author

Stacy Campbell is the author of *Dream Girl Awakened* and *Forgive Me*. She was born and raised in Sparta, Georgia, where she spent summers on her family's front porch listening to the animated tales of her older relatives. She lives with her family in Indianapolis, Indiana. You may visit the author: www.stacyloveswriting.com, georgiapeach2814@aol.com, www.facebook.com/stacy.campbell.376, and www.twitter.com/stacycampbell20